THE FALL OF PRINCES

❖ ❖ ❖

Also by Robert Goolrick

FICTION

A Reliable Wife

Heading Out to Wonderful

MEMOIR

The End of the World as We Know It

The Fall of Princes

❖ ❖ ❖

a novel

ROBERT GOOLRICK

ALGONQUIN BOOKS OF CHAPEL HILL   2015

Published by
ALGONQUIN BOOKS OF CHAPEL HILL
Post Office Box 2225
Chapel Hill, North Carolina 27515-2225

a division of
WORKMAN PUBLISHING
225 Varick Street
New York, New York 10014

LIBRARY OF CONGRESS
CATALOGING-IN-PUBLICATION DATA
Goolrick, Robert, [date]
The fall of princes : a novel / by Robert Goolrick.—First edition.
pages ; cm
ISBN 978-1-61620-420-4
I. Title.
PS3607.O5925F35 2015
813'.6—dc23   2015004191

10 9 8 7 6 5 4 3 2 1
First Edition

For
Billy Lux,
Who vanished,
and
Carolyn Marks Blackwood
and
Dana Martin Davis,
Who showed up

THE FALL OF PRINCES

❖ ❖ ❖

CHAPTER ONE

The Invention of Money

❖ ❖ ❖

When you strike a match, it burns brighter in the first nanosecond than it will ever burn again. That first incandescence. That instantaneous and brilliant flash. The year was 1980, and I was the match, and that was the year I struck into blinding flame.

I was a heat-seeking missile headed straight for your gut. Get out of the way or I would take you down. I swear. I'm not proud of it. In fact, I flush with shame at the memory. But that was then, what then was like. Things are very different now. I'm not that person anymore.

Then, I was the still, hot point of light at the end of the matchstick on which everything and everybody converged.

I could be seen clearly from outer space, a hot bright whiteness moving without guilt or pity through the hottest, brightest city in the world, and if you happened to be on a space walk on any given night, you could have had a front-row seat to my public chicaneries and my private excesses. Under the $1,000 duvet, on the $15,000 mattress, in the marble-tiled shower, slipping into a bespoke black cashmere jacket on a snowy winter night, I was unmistakable in my vast illumination.

Thousands of hours in the world's most expensive gym, with the world's most skilled trainers, had brought my body to such a state of perfection that the women who rushed to take off their clothes in my bedroom could only gasp at the luck that had put them into my line of sight, that had made them, even for one night, the most beautiful creatures on earth, with their lithe arms and their skin like chamois and their scents, God, their scents, and their golden manes of hair, falling on their shoulders, sweeping my chest. A glance was all it took from me. They could feel the heat, the hunger grew before they even knew my name, and they didn't care, they didn't care if I was an ax murderer or the Bishop of Lyons.

BSD. That was the phrase somebody coined to describe us and only us. "Big Swinging Dick"—and it stuck, and we wore that sobriquet like a badge of honor, and we sold our junk bonds and our trash securities, and made a $100,000 every microsecond of every minute, the match flaring into atomic glow, lighting up our faces, our ruddy cheeks or glinting eyes, our megawatts of greed and glory and rapaciousness.

My feet solidly on the ground in shoes from John Lobb in London, my legs mammoth, able to press three hundred pounds, able to leap tall buildings at a single bound, the rest going on from there, the powerful hips and haunches connected to a stomach as flat and hard as a frozen lake, yet hot to the touch, and they didn't care if they got burned or scarred for life, like junkies who can't stop until all the dope is gone, knowing that there is no more, that the withdrawal will be agony but not caring, yearning only for the sharp prick of the needle of my incandescent self.

I say this without pride or apology. It is a statement of irrefutable fact. I could charm a hatchling out of its egg. I could sell ice cream to Eskimos. Dead Eskimos.

And we worked. We worked our asses off. Before we came into the world, fully armed like Pallas Athene, work had somehow gone out of fashion, the men and women had become sluggish, their expectations limited, the horizon they had once envisioned lined with palaces and gorgeous objects of all kinds had become nothing more than a thin line in a rapidly approaching distance, the place they would end up, neither richer nor wiser, filled only with regret and second-tier liquor and the shreds of the dreams they no longer even remembered, surprised to wake up one day and be shown the door with a tepid handshake and a future on the edge of old age and death that held only pictures of the kids and grandkids, a cruise to some out-of-season destination every three years, and the notion, which they somehow managed to believe, that this was comfort, that this was all the splendor they got for forty years of relentless drudgery and obsequiousness.

And to all of this we said fuck you, we want it all, we want it now, you can drain us of our blood for all we care, but we want impossible things of impossible vintage and provenance. We want salaries equivalent to our ages multiplied by 100,000. We want to live life in a rush of fury and light, to rampage, to pillage our neighborhoods and rape and demolish our best and closest friends, and we were secure in this, knowing that, if we all wanted the same thing, everybody would get equally glorified and decimated. We were magnificent in our generosity, and stingy with our secret selves. We sang the executioner's song on our way to the office in the hour before dawn, and we spent our days playing high-stakes one-on-one basketball with other people's money in darkened rooms with no clocks so there was no compass, no marker, save for the hum of money, with other young men just like us, our inner lives obscured by insatiable greed, and we let our increasingly dubious virtues grow tangled and overgrown with layer after layer of objects, things, always things, suits that cost more than our fathers had paid for their first houses, cars of exuberant finesse, and the mountains of speeding tickets we got racing out to the East End of Long Island, where we kept the pools heated year-round.

We slept like babies at night.

And I walked through these crowds of men, all of whom wanted exactly what I wanted, and I beat them down until I was a colossus, and rather than inspire fear and loathing, they adored me, they wanted and sought my company, knowing that I would slam-dunk them off the court every single time, and then, like an abusive father, I would shower them with presents, gold watches, cashmere sweaters, and the gift of my smile, the perfect teeth, wholly created by Dr. Gregg Lituchy of Central Park South.

It was going to end. It had to. The worm would, in fact, devour its own tail, eat its own heart out, but that was of no consequence. Not then. Not at that time. Not to me.

Want to know how I got my job? How it all began? It wouldn't happen this way today. Today, you'd be hired based on some secret CEO algorithm that takes into account your Best in Show at Wharton, your height and your wing span, the charitable work you did in Guatemala when you were sixteen, your ethnic variety. Or maybe you're hired these days just because you haven't committed a major felony yet.

In those days, in the year of my incandescence, to get one of the most coveted jobs on Wall Street, you played poker. Winner take all. Job or no job based solely on your ability to beat the CEO at a hand of cards. That's not how it begins now. Not by a long shot. But then, one hand of poker is what sealed the deal.

It begins when you're in graduate school. You are courted, warily, at a distance. You feel them circling, and then they come closer, you can feel them breathing down your neck. You feel gifted, blessed, chosen. Then they strike, second year. You get the call that everybody in your class has been waiting for. The Firm, the legend and the gravitas and the money are on the other end of the line, and they are speaking to you in a polite, reserved tone of voice. So much is unspoken, so much unsaid but known. You are invited to New York to work your guts out for one summer, doing the drudge work, crunching numbers for eighteen hours a day. It is understood you will not be paid. This is never said. You pack your bags.

You are met at the train station by a young woman, snugly filling a sober but chic suit, knowing she will never get far in what was then an almost all male world. She got a

4.0 at the Darden School. Every minute of her life she has been the smartest person in the room and, at twenty-three, she is already facing a dead end, the certain knowledge that, however well she does, there is no future for her except a line in bold type on a résumé. She will never be paid what the boys are paid, but, in the end, she will be fine. She will move to Chase by twenty-five, where her every move will be applauded, the hinges of every door oiled to a whispering forgiveness by that one line in bold type that says she worked at The Firm. However briefly. She will retire with a ton of bucks, and a solid collection of good jewelry, and the husband and the three children and the house in Greenwich.

Now, she meets interns, fresh-faced, totally ignorant, crisp as a newly minted bill. She arranges for a porter, although you insist you don't need one. There is a way things are done in this world, and that way, even though you are a meaningless blob of nothingness, does not include carrying your own luggage. She leads you to a black town car, the first of hundreds, thousands of such cars you are to come to know, to take as your due. This, at The Firm, is what they call public transportation.

You are taken to an apartment in Murray Hill that you do not know then is the dreariest neighborhood in the whole of New York, dark, drab Murray Hill, and you are led into a large and pristine apartment where you are to spend the summer with three other guys who only yesterday were snapping each other's butts with wet towels in the locker rooms of the finest schools in the world, but who now stand in cordovan bluchers polished to sanctity, and pinstriped suits, their faces eager with greed and fear. Many are called but few are chosen, and you all know that, know also that most of you will never make it, will work your ass off for free for a single summer and then go back to the books and wait for a phone call that does not ever come. This is where it begins, this sizing up, the eying of the jugular.

Then the real courtship begins. You have never been fawned over. You are now. You are watched, and the watchers are swooning. They love you, with an adoration that is both sensual and pragmatic. You are merely another potential ROI to them, but you feel their love, their lust for what you can do for them. You grow taller, stronger, handsomer. You have your shoes polished every day. You arrive every morning so pressed, so starched, that you could shave with the edge of your shirt collar, and by eleven you are a rumpled wreck, because that only makes them love you more, the dishevelment of relentless labor.

They take you around the harbor on Malcolm Forbes's boat, *The Highlander,* white-coated waiters bring you icy, sweating Heinekens as the Statue of Liberty serenely observes this year's crop of immigrants, and you want to get shit-faced but you don't, and you want to sleep with the trim women but you don't, out of fear that their inevitable doom and departure will leave you scarred, will infect you with their own failure. One in a hundred of them will make it into The Firm, one in a thousand will make it upstairs, one in a million has the mark of the BSD. Unfair. Maybe. But you didn't make the rules.

They take you to the theater, center orchestra, on the aisle, to watch ludicrous spectacles for which not one single ticket is available for the next two years. They take you to Yankee Stadium, to Shea, where the heroes of your childhood are so close you can see the stubble on their chins. You see Madonna at the Garden, this girl who has caught the zeitgeist and sucked the world into the profound depth of her vagina, this BSD chick who seems to look into your eyes only and she opens her mouth and electrifies you with her power, as though she would not fade, like Cleopatra, not ever, as though the strike of the match was for her and only her, an infinity.

There are twenty interviews, formal, identical except for the fact that the offices get larger each time you are called to trot out your brilliant résumé. You speak of nothing else but your ambition. They talk about the culture of success, a culture you must not only thrive in, you must become, historical.

The questions get more pointed, more personal with every interview. Do you do drugs? Have you ever cheated on a test? Lied to the IRS? Are you a homosexual? What do you dream about while you sleep? Do you ever have thoughts of suicide? Patently illegal questions, even then, but you answer, and you tell the truth because you know they already know the answers and would spot a lie a mile off.

It's like being tested for rabies, except that, in this case, they're only looking for positive results. Only the rabid dogs, the ones who have been starved and beaten with chains, teeth filed to ice picks, killer dogs to be put in the ring to kill other dogs, only these pass the interviews and move on to the next, bigger room.

Do you hate your parents?

Have you ever gotten a girl pregnant? What did you do about it?

How often do you masturbate? Would you consider that excessive?

You feel as though you are standing naked at Dachau, inspected by uniformed Gestapo who are deciding which line you are to join. And everybody smiles through it all. Everybody speaks in a kind, almost loving voice as they invade your every orifice, begin the arduous task of taking over your mind and melding it into what they repeatedly call "the culture" of The Firm.

Forty or forty, they say with a smile. Forty or forty. Excuse me?

That's when you retire, they reply with that bland smile. When you reach the age of forty, or your portfolio reaches forty million. That's when you can get away clean and get your life back. What's left of it.

Bulls make money, they say. Bears make money. Pigs get slaughtered. They tell you these things, and you instantly know in your heart what they mean, and it speaks to your heart and your gut in a way no voice ever has.

They tell you these things, and you believe them. You can reach into your pocket and feel the weight of $40 million, not even a hint of gray at your temples yet, and your life stretching before you, the golden door, the brilliant road, the Ithaca, as Cavafy wrote, to which you have journeyed all these years.

The summer ends. They shake your hand and say they will see you again, although everybody knows this is only marginally true.

In November, the call comes. Tickets are sent, first class, the train station, the porters and the trim and futureless girl, the black car that drives you all the way downtown to the black glass tower where the black car pulls into a group of black cars just like it, lined up around the block three deep.

This is your future. Or it isn't.

You walk with confidence into the CEO's office. Your handshake is warm, your hands dry, your grip so firm the muscles on your forearm ripple as you take it all in, the sleek desk with nothing on it, the model of the yacht he undoubtedly owns, 120 feet of yar, his $20,000 watch, the bespoke suit, the look back into your eyes that says he likes you but would nevertheless kill you without the slightest hesitation.

Your coat is taken by one of his eight secretaries, a young woman who looks as though she is the princess of a not minor European country, and the coat is put on a hanger as though it is an exhibit in a museum and whisked out of sight. The office has been decorated by Mark Hampton to look like a drawing room in an English country house, and you know instantly that no business is ever done in here, that all of that takes place somewhere else so that nothing in this chintz and mahogany world is ever disturbed by so much as a raised voice.

On the desk once owned by Napoleon is a single thing— a deck of cards on which the seal has not even been broken.

"The furniture is real," he says. "Try not to stick your gum on it."

"My résumé," you say, reaching into your portfolio from T. Anthony.

"Fuck that," he says. Your résumé has been seen more times than *Gone with the Wind*. "You're not the smartest, you're not the dumbest. I know everything about you. I know you slept with Suzanne Martin, who was much smarter than you, and who no longer works here. No, résumés are for other people.

"Here's what's going to happen," he says. "We're going to play a hand of poker. One hand. You win, you get a job. You lose, sayonara."

"Yes, sir."

"At the end of the game, you will be given your coat and you will leave. On your way out, you will be given a box. Inside the box, there will be a Montblanc pen. You will also be given a notebook. Once you leave, you will sign your name in the book. The ink will be either blue or black. All contracts are signed in blue ink.

"We're going to play an unusual version of showdown. Rare, but not unheard of. I am going to lay all fifty-two cards face up on the desk. Total transparency. That, too, is part of the culture you may or may not be entering. You pick first. You can pick any five cards you want. After we've drawn, we both can discard and replace as many cards as we want once we've seen both our hands. But I have to tell you, there is a hand, one hand, and only one hand, that will ensure that you win, no matter what I pick. Ready?"

"Yes, sir."

We both stare at the cards, laid out so neatly, four straight rows of thirteen, on Napoleon's desk. Suddenly, it comes to me. I wait, brow furrowed, then tentatively reach out, withdraw, and finally pick. I want to show uncertainty, although I know already I've won the bet. In less than a minute, I'll be one of them. Is it even what I want? I don't know. In that moment, I feel the music lessons, the life-drawing classes, the college theatricals. The self I had meant to be. I had wanted to be an artist, to express something that was inside me that needed to be said. The fact that I hadn't a clue as to what that thing was didn't deter me at all in the beginning. I worked hard and was terrible at everything. I wrote a bad novel, painted bad pictures, plodded through plays, parts I could speak but never inhabit, until I had had enough and I decided, if I couldn't be eloquent, at least I could be rich. Beauty was too ephemeral and elusive. Money, that year, was the most tangible avatar of the zeitgeist, and not to grab it would be to miss the common experience of your generation. I thought it would protect me from the disappointment I felt in my own many and varied failures. I couldn't be what I wanted to be, a maker of beauty, and so I took my father's advice and went to business school, and caught it like a fever, the pulse of the money that was being made in my country, and I wanted in, because no place else would have me. I could, I thought, work among them and not become one of them. I was sensitive, poetic, and vulnerable to life's beauty, and now I sat on the other side of a desk that once belonged to Napoleon, one draw of the cards away from the devil. I hated abandoning the dreams of my youth, but in that second, the one thing I want is to win. I draw four tens and the three of hearts. I would learn to play the cello when I was old and finished with all of this. Paint watercolors of seascapes out of season. Act in local theater companies, playing the small parts, the butler, the next-door neighbor, grease paint and footlight bows.

The Man looks at me across the desk. He smiles, and draws a nine high straight flush, spades in a row, ostensibly beating my four of a kind. But I know and he knows he can't get a straight flush higher than nine, because I have all the tens. I've blocked him by drawing them all. Nine is as high as he can go. He knows it, too, not that anything, anything, shows in his face. He's done this hundreds of times.

I discard everything but the ten of hearts, and draw the jack, queen, king, and ace of hearts for a royal flush.

We stare at each other for a long time. The game is done. The cards are laid on the desk without a word from either of us.

"That concludes the interview. Thank you for coming."

We stand, shake hands. He is either my new boss or just someone I met once in an ostentatious office in my youth.

The secretary hands me a box wrapped in white paper

with a white satin ribbon making a bow. She also hands me a notebook of blank pages, bound in leather, with the firm's name embossed at the top and my name embossed in smaller letters in the lower right-hand corner. My name is spelled correctly.

"Good luck," she says, as she has said a thousand times before.

I wait until I'm on the train before I open the box. I take out the black-and-gold pen with the familiar logo on the cap and open the notebook and sign my name in royal blue ink.

Pay attention. You can hear the match strike. You can smell the sulfur, and I allow myself the slightest smile as the train pulls out of the station through the dark tunnels and into the brilliance of the future.

CHAPTER TWO

Belated

❖   ❖   ❖

Forgive me.

I try not to think about the past very much. The way it was and isn't anymore. I try to, you know, go with the flow and live my life as it's handed to me. But sometimes I wake from a dream and I can't help it. The past washes over me like the tides and along with the tides comes a sense of mortification so profound I feel it in my scrotum, like when you're thinking about the likelihood of having your teeth drilled.

Forgive me for thinking that I was better than you will ever be. Forgive me for thinking that money equaled a kind of moral superiority. Forgive me for not thinking enough about the plight of the poor, the terrible lassitude that overtakes them the moment their feet hit the floor. The poor only bet on losing horses. They only give up things, they never get, until there's nothing left to part with, nothing of any value except for a faded photograph of their mother and father's wedding, a small figurine given to them on the boardwalk on one happy day in a lifetime of unending sameness.

And they never look at the fiber content of the clothes they buy at Walmart. And they have a fear of running out of things, out of butter, out of sugar, out of laundry detergent. And they suffer nothing but one humiliation after another and they buy scratchers with their welfare money at the gas station and they never win a dime.

For poor people, it's always Christmas Eve. Alone. Christmas never comes.

And then there's AIDS, or the homeless who wait for volunteers to come and dish out a bland Thanksgiving dinner, or food stamps, or bad teeth or being ugly. Forgive me for thinking that these were things that happened to other people on another planet.

Forgive me, Blonde Girl, for going to the men's room between dinner and dessert, stopping to pay the check with the maitre d', grabbing my coat and walking out of the restaurant on a snowy February night to hail a cab and go to a loud, hot room where the people were more attractive.

How long did you sit there? How long did you endure the pitying condescension of the waiters? How did it feel to leave the restaurant and stand with the snow falling and nowhere to go, the careful makeup, the sequined dress all for nothing in the night, for this insult, and barely enough money in your purse to get home to your flat crowded with girls just like you?

You had perfect legs. The curve of your breasts beneath the gauzy dress was sublime. You paid three hundred dollars to have your hair colored. And for what? To be left alone in the middle of the restaurant of the week, by a man who doesn't even remember your name? By a man who never gave it a second thought until the lonely nights descended without expiation.

Who told the story later over and over as though it were some joke and you were the punch line.

Forgive me for thinking that sitting courtside at the Knicks at four hundred a pop, three seats away from Spike Lee, was a useful way of spending money. Forgive me for thinking that meeting a movie star was the same as knowing movie stars, perhaps the most unknowable people on earth.

The truth is, I had no deep respect and took no pride in what I did, I just did it for fun and the high, the restless high roll of it all, and so the money I made meant nothing to me. There was no time, no future. There were only piles of cash. I felt no particular compunction about manipulating the hopes of people less fortunate than myself, people who would never hold the reins of a Derby winner in their hands, as I did every day, all day long.

It's three a.m. and sleep will not come. There are too many ghosts in the room. I don't dwell in the past, as I said, but tonight I'm there again, right there, with the roll and the flow and the vulgar indiscretions and the unbridled narcissism of it all. I'm buried in guilt and remorse. I am overcome with rage that the past is over, irrevocably, that I have my laundry done at the wash and fold, that I know exactly how much it costs to buy a pint of half-and-half for my coffee, that the men and women I spent so many years with are lost to me forever. The darlings of my youth. They speak a different language. I have forgotten the way, the argot, the inflection. I am sad that the places I used to drink and dance and eat and whore are now just numbers in somebody else's Filofax.

I see the past, I feel its addictions, but the faces are indistinct and the voices are mute. The past is only the place you came home to one day to find the locks changed, the rooms stripped of furniture, of every object from which you had derived such ridiculous amounts of self-esteem.

Do they ever think of me? I doubt they do. There are, after all, more interesting topics. Success has a million musical nuances. Failure is only the monotonous banging of a brass gong.

Forgive me, French girl I met while she was bathing topless on the beach at the Delano Hotel. Frank bet me I couldn't fuck her by ten o'clock, bet me a hundred dollars I couldn't have sex with her by the time we met for dinner, and I showed up at ten with the girl on my arm and said, "You lose," and Frank gave me a hundred right in front of her.

She was staying at a cheesy motel, and she'd only come to the Delano to meet nice rich men. Men like me. When I put her on the plane, she looked at me with fear.

Forgive me for thinking I was good-hearted. I wasn't. For thinking even now that nevertheless God has a special place in his heart for me, that there is a reason for all this suffering.

Forgive me for thinking that black limousines were public transportation.

This night will last forever. I am locked in the darkness until the end of time. I have reached the age of regret, and forgive me my hour of lamentation and self-pity.

We used to go to this sports bar all the time where we would eat bad food and drink endless cocktails and dip the tips of our cigars in snifters of Remy and watch sports on TV. We played a game, night after night for a while.

The game was called To Have and To Have Not. The idea was you had to think of something you had done that nobody else at the table had done, or something you had never done that everybody else had done. You had to tell the truth. It was understood.

If you could think of something that made you unique, everybody toasted you and took a drink, although, since we were drinking pretty much continuously, the toasts were pretty much pro forma.

The early nights, the entries were mostly sexual.

"I've had sex on the pitcher's mound at the University of Denver." Unremarkably enough, her fiancé blushingly had to admit that he had, too.

"I've been in a threeway." Practically everybody.

"I've masturbated at a movie."

"In the theater or at home watching a porno?"

"In the theater."

It turns out, a lot of people have masturbated at the movies, mostly when they were teenagers. This is something that happens, the huge, glowing image, the sensual mouths, the whispered dialogue. Somehow, it's all sexual, sitting in the dark.

But once the usual sexual shenanigans were out of the way, the entries got both more commonplace and more fascinating. It took weeks until people's real distinguishing peculiarities began to appear, but, when they did, it was pretty riveting.

We would sit around all day, trying to think of some minor detail of our lives that would make us drinkably unique.

Dan said, "I've never been swimming. Never even been in the water." Everybody drank.

June said one night, "I've never tasted beer," and this was a woman who owned a Mexican restaurant and could pack it away with the best of them.

Teddy said, "I've never taken a photograph." We couldn't believe it.

Then, one night, after a long dry spell, I put out a sure-fire winner. "I've had sex with an animal."

By this time we were pretty much past the stage of being shocked at the vagaries of human behavior, but this did raise an eyebrow or two and people started to lift their glasses when crisp, fastidious Teddy suddenly said, "So have I."

Glasses down and general discussion of where and why and how it worked and so forth, but one of the rules by then was that nothing got discussed very much. You didn't have to explain yourself, you just had to stand out from the herd.

It came to be my turn again and I said, "I've had a girl kill herself because I dumped her." And Teddy again said, "So have I," and all discussion stopped and we hardly ever played the game again. Too many cats were out of too many bags and I had upped the ante beyond most people's willingness to reveal their secrets in the middle of a musty sports bar.

Imagine two people having those same identical experiences; it's outside the realm of possibility or thought.

Forgive me my callousness with the details of my life, with the intimacies of other people's.

The girl who killed herself was tall. She was twenty-four. So was I. We had been sweethearts in college and then we had broken up while I went to business school, and then we had gotten together when we were both in the city.

She got pregnant, and I paid for an abortion, and then I dumped her. I had just gone to work, thrilling in the fact that somebody paid you basically to play one-on-one basketball all day long, and I didn't want her around anymore. I wanted the world. But I didn't want her. She was too small. She was too fresh.

She wrote me a note, which I still have, and then she slit her wrists in the bathtub. Her parents were deeply mournful and couldn't figure out why she had done it. I guess you never do.

I never told them about the note or the pregnancy or the many ways in which I had longed to be free of her.

I can't even say her name. I remember everything about her, I remember her softness and her light-heartedness and the way she loved me. I remember her in my prayers and there is no amount of forgiveness that will undo what I did.

She was my last soft girlfriend. And I used her as a show-stopper in a bar game.

The child would be almost thirty by now, a fine young person, I imagine, with a whole clean life, like untracked snow.

I would be a better person. I wouldn't be alone. There would be a card and a call on my birthday. In the middle of the night, I hear his voice, it's always him, never her, I wouldn't have known what to do with a girl, and he says, "Hi, Dad," a way of addressing your father my mother would have considered tacky, and I feel the warmth spreading in my heart.

She was tall, as I said, the girl whose name I won't say, even to myself, even at three in the morning, in the dark, in my apartment where everything speaks of loss, where everything I have reminds me of everything I used to have, as though there were still a gold Rolex on the night table, the key to a Mercedes CLK still on my bureau on its silver keychain from Tiffany's, the Schnabel on the wall, whereas in actuality none of these things exist, or exist in places to which I have no access, the vintage-watch-store window, the storage bins at Christie's waiting for the market for Schnabel to come back.

"Hi, Dad." How much that would have meant to me, now. My birthday goes unmarked. I buy myself a birthday cake, even have it decorated with my name on top, and I have a slice after I eat my takeout sushi at the kitchen table. You still do these little things for yourself because not to do them would mean that you had simply ceased to exist. You have to pretend, when speaking to the ladies in the cake store, that the cake is for a friend, pretend that you're giving a big party so you need the cake that serves twenty, and you sit at the kitchen table with this enormous and elaborate cake for twenty with your name written in fondant on the top, and you feel worse about yourself than you ever have in your life, but, after the sushi box has been thrown out and the stray drops of soy sauce have been wiped from the Formica table top and the dishes, what few there are, have been washed and put away because you have to hold on to some kind of order or you are lost altogether, you sit down and put a single candle on the cake you bought for yourself and light it and make a wish before blowing it out, and then you cut a big piece of the immense cake and you eat it and you sob as the too-sweet dessert goes into your mouth. I buy myself a tie for my birthday, and have it wrapped, and I open my present and mime surprise, all the while waiting for the phone to ring and the voice on the other end to say, "Hi, Dad."

I am so sorry. My sorrow is immense, bigger than the cake, gaudier than the paper wrapping the drab tie.

I wash the plate and the fork, and put them away, and then I put the rest of the cake back into the box and drop it down the garbage chute for the rats. Happy birthday, rats.

Hi Dad's tall mother, an inch taller than I am, and as beautiful as the Blue Ridge Mountains in April, and she had come to New York to be a ballerina, but her height had proved to be a problem. While dancing, she appeared to be not graceful but merely astonishing, and nobody could figure out what to do with her. Even the great Balanchine was baffled. He tried. Her form, he said, was exquisite, but she towered over the boys, and the lifts always ended in some comic disaster, so he turned her away with his usual coldness. She was useless to him, and therefore of no interest, except possibly in bed, where he was already overbooked for the season.

So she turned to modeling. She trudged the streets of the city with her portfolio, listening again and again to the list of her flaws. She shaved off her eyebrows, in an attempt to separate herself from the other girls who, like her, were almost there but not quite. This did not make her more beautiful; it just gave her a look of continual surprise so that it seemed that everything that came out of your mouth was the most fascinating thing she had ever heard.

The most beautiful feature of a beautiful woman is her skin. After all, that's what you touch. Her skin had a kind of clammy, plastic quality to it, so my desire for her was mixed with a kind of simultaneous repulsion. Sometimes, or at least sometimes in those days, I would find myself crazy with desire for a woman who also repelled me, and that would drive me to heights of lust unknown with ordinary women. Not that I slept with many ordinary women. I remember them all, every one, and I think of each of them every day, and always with love and gratitude in my heart. So grateful that they would let me take off my clothes and lie next to them, actually to enter them and become one with their bodies.

We squabbled all the time, and every time we had a fight, we would go and have our hair cut, so, in our few moments of uneasy truce, between her look of shocked beauty and mine of profligate prosperity, we could pretty much stop traffic on any street corner, just for our gorgeous heads of hair alone, get past any velvet rope because we adorned any room we were in. I was crazy about her. I couldn't stand her most of the time, but I was crazy about her. As for her, she was "high-strung," as my mother used to say and almost impossible to live with.

"You don't love me," she said one day.

"But I do," I lied. "I do love you."

"Well, you don't love me *enough*!" she yelled back, and

thought to myself, Define that, please. When is enough enough? But, for her, as they say in Texas, "Too much ain't enough."

So we broke up. I had met a photographer, a rich, good photographer who looked, in her retro way, like Tamara de Lempicka. She lived on a large allowance from her mother, who had buckets of money from her second husband, and came to our relationship with Tiffany silver for twenty-four, and that Tiffany china that has a black border with chinoiserie painted around it, also for twenty-four, and I wanted her like the desert wants rain, and I broke up with the eyebrow girl.

"We're turning into the kind of people I don't want to be," I said. And left her at her kitchen table, this time genuinely surprised. She had thought our life, fighting like two cats in a bag and then making love that would cause the angels to sing, was just fine.

Photographer and I moved in together. Her mother was on everybody's best-dressed list, at least in Philadelphia, and she had an attic full of couture clothes dating back to the fifties and had Norman Norell's home number in her phone book, and the photographer spent her days taking magical pictures of her friends in her mother's clothes and showed them at a very prestigious gallery. She took my picture naked for my thirtieth birthday, and of all the girls and all the detritus of all those liaisons, it is the best of the souvenirs I keep. Just a look at it and it all comes back to me and I just stare and say I'm sorry over and over and over. I owe them all my most sincere apology, but as occasionally happens, if I pass one of them on the street, they invariably look at me with such hatred that I am frightened to speak to them. Sometimes they have husbands and babies with them, and I think of my child, which I learned about in a message left on my answering machine.

We met. She claimed I owed her a hundred dollars for some reason, and an abortion. I gave her the money, and I arranged everything, and took her in at seven one morning and waited in the waiting room, learning household tips like how to keep your stockings from running by keeping them in the freezer, about how to polish your dining room table with mayonnaise, and then it was over, and she left with me and I put her in a cab, still surprised, and we never saw each other or spoke again.

I wept at the funeral, where her great and magnificent height was reduced to ashes in a box eight inches square. Death reduces us so. On the way out of the church, after saying hello to her large and universally tall family, I stopped to talk to a mutual friend, well, her best friend, actually, who asked why I was crying so much, and I confessed it was not so much for her as for my lost child. I wanted children.

She got scattered into the sea off of Montauk Point and

I went for a stint at Miss Valentine Lutrell's Home for Persons Who Have Lost Their Minds, Either Through Negligence, Recklessness, or Theft. I was there for eight weeks, and didn't get a single phone call, except from my mother, who said, "What did you do this time?" and I hung up on her. As though, whatever I had done, I had done it to her, and did it all the time.

I don't have such a bad record, if you ask me. It's funny about being in the slammer. I've been four times, twice in rehab for various addictions, and twice to the loony bin. Not a bad record for somebody my age. I look at it like taking the car in to be serviced before the engine burns or freezes, whatever engines do.

So, the cake eaten and now suffering the trampling and gnawing of rats, the tie hung up with the dozens of others, I sit and wait for my son to call. Over the years, I have taken possession of him or he of me, and I have watched him grow, and never missed a Little League game or a school play. Hi, Dad. He's a good man. Grown now, and married.

The phone, however, will not ring, will never ring, except a call from some telemarketers whom I will engage in conversation until they are sure I am a lunatic and sign off.

Other than that, what is there to offer you by way of reparations? A tiny parting of the curtain. Her name was Diana. Her name at birth was Dianne, but she changed it.

She pictured it on a marquee, on a magazine cover, and Diana just seemed more elegant. Another surprise.

And mine? My name? It hardly matters. When I go to work now, it's on the nametag I am forced to wear. Ever since 9/11, wearing a name tag gives me the willies. Once my name was on my license plate. But nobody even looks at my name tag, and the ladies who write my name on my birthday cake have forgotten it before the icing sets. I know it comes late in the game, but the only thing that matters is what I would say after my son called to say Hi, Dad.

I'm sorry.

CHAPTER THREE

Give Me Liberty or Give Me Death

❖ ❖ ❖

Wh   hen it came time to fire me, it took our
               man behind Napoleon's desk, three peo-
               ple from HR, my immediate supervisor,
and four lawyers. I could hardly blame them. They had done
everything they could. It started with good, sound advice,
then formal counseling, then two rehabs, three fat files of
"incidents," as they called them, and finally, a meeting in
the Big House where nothing had changed since the cards
were first dealt, except that the model of the yacht had been
replaced by a bigger model of an even bigger yacht, one
hundred and sixty-two feet of teak. All this so that I could
be summoned bright and early, seven in the morning, to a

meeting where the only thing that was to be said of substance was two words.

It was on a Thursday. It's always on a Thursday, so you have a long weekend to kill yourself.

I stood there, the exact model of the white collar drunk and addict, clean-shaven, buffed nails, whacked out of my skull.

The silence lasted what seemed like an eternity, not a movement, not a breath, as my grandmother used to say on particularly hot days. Finally, The Man spoke.

"You're fired," he said.

I didn't flinch. The sweat on my back was soaking through my $5,000 suit. The HR people took notes, the lawyers looked at their own reflections in their highly polished shoes.

"Do you want to know why?" he said.

I didn't speak or move.

"Do. You. Want. To. Know. Why." His voice was rising perceptibly.

"Of what possible use would that be to me?" I answered.

"Then get out of my office," he yelled, causing me, for the first time, to flinch.

I walked out. The eight secretaries did not look up at me. They were embarrassed. I heard his voice behind me, yelling for real now.

"Wait! You! Get back in here!"

I stopped. "No," I said. "I don't think I feel like that. I'm not doing it."

The secretaries, all eight of them, now looked up at me, horrified. Nobody had ever said no before. Not to that voice.

"Yes, you are," he said forcefully. "If you ever want to work on the Street again, you'll get your ass back in this office this second."

I knew he was right. I turned and walked back into the office. He got up from behind his desk and came around to my side.

He stood in front of me, glaring at me with bald hatred in his eyes. I had a good eight inches on him, but, somehow, he stared at me at eye level. We stood. We just stood, him bristling with loathing, me sweating so heavily it ran down my cheeks and dripped onto my Charvet tie.

How long did it last? Two minutes? Three? Whatever. It went on for a long time.

He erupted like Vesuvius, spewing venom and spit as a volcano spews lava. I have never heard a voice like that, before or, thank God, after.

"NOW GET THE *FUCK* OUT OF MY OFFICE!"

Manners are such an elusive thing. Once you have them, they are on you like your skin. You have them all the time, every hour of every day, and they never leave you bereft.

Outside his thirty-eighth-floor office, there was a sudden swirl of brilliant birds, brilliant colors, soaring and drifting, so alive, so precious in their gentle beauty, driven, in the early morning light, to fly with joy in unimaginably beautiful patterns. My only wish at that moment, was that I could jump through the window and join them, dazzle with color and swoop, before I fell all thirty-eight floors to land on top of one of the black cars waiting, as they eternally did, on the street.

Instead, I held out my hand. I actually thrust out my arm to shake his hand in farewell.

He slapped me in the face.

I left his office, leaving behind my last shred of dignity, my one triumphant gesture. I left, and I left behind a life that had once been mine and would never be mine again.

How sad, how beautifully elegant the swoon of birds.

CHAPTER FOUR

The Sweetheart of My Youth

❖ ❖ ❖

My wife Carmela divorced me the day I got fired. Despite the fact that we loved each other with our whole hearts, and had lived together for five years before we got married in a half-million-dollar wedding in East Hampton, only a year before, with both Lee Radziwill and Henry Kissinger in attendance. She was a smart girl, and she could easily see when the last card in the deck had been played.

At our wedding reception, on the dunes, in front of the house we had been given as a wedding present, klieg lights had been shone on the ocean so the guests could see the breakers rolling in, just for us.

She wanted everything, loft, furniture, art. I gave it to her with a glad heart. She was used to nice things, and I loved her and I had nice things, so I just let her take it all. When the guy came to serve me the papers, I knew what they said before I opened them, and, still, all I could think of was my love for her, the only real love I had ever known, and I wished her all the best even as I saw that she intended never to see me again.

The broken wall, the burning roof and tower
And Agamemnon dead

The details haunted me as I read the document. Never again would we hire a caterer and white-coated waiters to host dinners for twenty-four. We would never tandem water ski in St. Barth's. Worst of all, we ended without issue, as they say. I would never have the children who would adore me and warm my old age. My youth ended in that moment.

She gave me twenty-four hours to get my personal effects—I love that phrase, like something out of a murder crime scene: "to get my personal effects"—out of the apartment. She went to stay at the Plaza, and have lunch at Grenouille with her mother, who was practiced at the art of divorce, having done it three times.

Fanelli, my raucous but lovable coworker and my best friend, called. "Here's what we do. Get three rolls of quarters, meet me at some dive bar, and we drink ourselves stupid in the daytime while you call every headhunter and contact you have in town. In the world. London. Geneva. Tokyo. We'll get you set. Don't worry."

And so we did. All those quarters dropping into the box. The phone ringing and ringing, the polite secretaries who greeted me as though I were a brother home from the war, yet refused to put my calls through to whoever it was I needed to speak to.

I had gone from BSD to almost a nonperson when The Man slapped my face, a story that racketed through the whole game, so that everybody knew it within an hour. I had been the most valuable bull in the pen. Suddenly I was horsemeat, headed for the slaughterhouse, and nobody would take my calls.

Ever again. That much was clear. Crystal.

Carmela had heard about it from her stepfather before the swirling birds came to roost, and he instructed her step by step about how to set out to leave me with nothing. The first thing she did was empty the joint bank accounts, leaving me only a small but secret stash in Grand Cayman, and put our money, once mine, then ours, now hers, securely in her name in her stepfather's bank. Then to the lawyer's (stopping on the way for a manicure and pedicure), where she was coached about what to do to ensure that there was nothing left in my name. She ran her perfectly manicured hands through her perfectly disarranged hair and signed document after document until there was nothing left to get.

I loved her with every cell of my being. She was in my brain and in my blood, and the loss of her was infinitely worse than the slap in the face. And I know she loved me. Or at least she loved me when I was on the come. And still. And still. She knew it, and I knew it. The ink in my pen had turned from blue to black, and whatever contracts had been signed, even promises made from the heart, whispered pillow to pillow in the night, were null and void.

I resented nothing. Didn't have the strength.

Why, what could she have done, being what she is?

Was there a second Troy for her to burn?

Irreconcilable differences. The two saddest words in the English language.

I called the movers, and watched as my beautiful things went onto racks and into boxes, suits and shirts and shoes that were worth the price of a house. I took the sheets, so beautiful they might have comprised a museum exhibit. I took the towels, monogrammed with my initials. I took the toothpaste.

All these things went to Hovel Hall, my rat-infested starter apartment, and as they entered the doors of that apartment, after climbing five flights of steps, you could see the disappointment and sympathy on the faces of the movers, and I tipped them overly generously so they could forget that they had ever been in those shabby rooms, seen the failure inherent in that sad move.

I looked around the apartment. Hopeless. I began to put my things away in the inadequate closets. A bad wind was rising, all of the world's seven malevolent winds were blowing in my heart, flattening and desiccating the landscape, once verdant, into a desert.

I had never loved anybody more than I loved Carmela at that moment. And I knew it was permanent. Romance, Inc., had shut its doors forever.

Forever.

CHAPTER FIVE

The Place I Really Live

❖ ❖ ❖

I wake up in the dark. *Au bout de la nuit*, 4:06 on the LED. Take a leak. Cigarette. I know I shouldn't; I mean, in general, generally speaking, nobody should, not after everything we know, not after we've watched loved ones die, not to mention movie stars, but I do. I'm an addict. But I especially shouldn't smoke at 4:06 when I have a hope of getting back to sleep. It makes my heart race.

It makes the heavy covers feel like prison garb. It makes you feel like you live in a cheap bungalow in Los Angeles, California, in a noir decade.

If I did live in Los Angeles, I would never call it L.A. But if I lived in Las Vegas, I would always call it Vegas.

These are the games your mind plays when it's 4:07 and your heart is racing from the nicotine intake.

I turn on the radio and listen to alternative rock from the University of Pennsylvania for a while. My Morning Jacket. Placebo. Ray LaMontagne, who used to work in a shoe factory. Pink Martini, a twelve-member West Coast band that sold 650,000 copies of their self-made CD from their basement.

I keep the volume low, and I feel completely free of anxiety, even though my heart is racing and I'm excited about tomorrow.

Tomorrow, or today, actually, is the first Tuesday of December. On the first Tuesday of every month, I go look at apartments.

I work at Barnes and Noble, and I have Monday and Tuesday off, since I work on Saturdays, and I work the late shift on Sundays, after I go to church. I go to church every week, and put money in the plate, even though I have long ago lost my faith. I guess it's a kind of hope I feel, a hope that faith and a sense of the miraculousness of life will return to me. It hasn't, and the priests' voices drone on in that way that is supposed to be comforting but is actually kind of irritating, but I still go. I sit, in one of my decades-old suits, in a sea of mink and the finest tailored wool, and then I go to work, still in my suit.

I am the only clerk in the store who wears hard-soled

shoes. Even though it makes my feet hurt, and even though nobody ever looks at my feet, I wear leather-soled shoes every day I work there. It makes me feel more like a member of the professional class, and less like somebody who just swipes your card. I'm very fastidious, and the kids in their Barnes and Noble T-shirts think it's weird, but I banter with them, banter is the word, and I know everything they know about alternative rock, and I'm good at helping them out with the inevitable glitches in their computer cash registers, and so we get along fine.

Let's not talk about what I do with my days off the other three weeks of the month. Let's not even get into that. I turn the phone off, for one thing, even though hardly anybody ever calls me, my sister from upstate once in a while, but let's not go into that.

I go to the grocery store and buy a whole week's worth of groceries, even though I mostly eat in the diner around the corner. I just like the way a full refrigerator looks, the endless possibilities. I pay for the groceries with my debit card. At the end of the week, I throw out stuff that's gone bad and go get other stuff.

I take the laundry to the wash and fold, the sheets to the Chinese lady who does them for me. I go to the Metropolitan Museum of Art and look at the same twelve paintings. I have a membership.

But it's all just normal. You probably do the same things, on your day off. Take your shirts to the laundry. Run an errand. Take a nap. Work in your woodworking shop, whatever your hobby is.

My hobby is looking at apartments I will never move into.

On Monday, I go in and make the appointment. I always dress well, not too well, not a suit or anything, but a nice blazer and a pair of trousers with double pleats, fresh from the dry cleaners so the pleats are razor-sharp.

They make you fill out an application; how much you make, what you're looking for, how much you're willing to spend. I always lie. I say that I'm a fashion retail executive. If they ask, I'll say I work at Saks. I put down that I make $375,000 a year. I put down an address where I do not live, and a phone number that is one digit off my real phone number. It's not like you have to show proof or anything. You could be anybody. Everybody does it, so you don't get the follow-up calls.

I GIVE THEM A fake name. Billy Champagne, a name I heard once in a locker room at a gym I used to belong to. This guy, Billy Champagne, was saying to a friend of his that the only reason he worked out so hard was he needed something to do with all his energy since he stopped drinking.

He said that he used to drink a quart of Scotch every day before lunch, down there on Wall Street, and everybody, I swear everybody in the locker room said "Jesus" under his breath at the same time, with a kind of hushed awe. Billy Champagne was this guy's name, he was built like a linebacker, he had a beautiful, powerful body, and the irony of it never left me, so I use his name. I like the name. I'd gladly *be* Billy Champagne, drunk or sober.

I tell them I'm willing to spend $4,500 a month on a one- or two-bedroom apartment. I say this, knowing they'll show me much more expensive apartments anyway. Or I say I'll also consider looking at lofts, live in a more open, abstract kind of way. I'd like to see as many apartments as possible on Tuesday, starting at ten a.m.

I don't go to the same realtor more than once every six months. Not that they care. Talk about hope. They live on hope. Hope and greed, those guys.

I lie awake in the dark for a long time. I smoke another Marlboro Red. You should see me smoke a cigarette. I do it with a voluptuous finesse. Then I put it out in my mother's silver ashtray and turn off the radio right after the U of P goes off the air when the Blue Nile has finished their incredibly moving "Because of Toledo." In the song, which pierces my heart every time, people talk about how lonely and misplaced they are. Like a girl in the song, just a girl, that's all we know about her, in this diner, I guess, who's leaning on a jukebox in some old blue jeans she wears. Saying wherever it is she lives she doesn't really live anywhere.

I could weep for that girl, a fictional desolation living her one spark of life in a diner in a city I've never been to. Then I hear the line from Shakespeare: "And I could sing, Would weeping do me good, / And never borrow any tear of thee."

At five thirty in the morning, the mind caroms around like a squash ball, hitting just above the line and then careening off in some totally unpredictable direction. You go from certain brilliance to absolute drudgery in a second. And, of course, it's Advent now, and after that comes Christmas, so there's that, too. I'd lean on that jukebox with that girl and tell her to cheer the hell up. She has no special claim to desolation, in my view.

I go back to sleep until seven thirty. I've been awake for an hour and a half.

When I wake up, I'm groggy and I'm still tired, but I'm also excited, the way I always am. It's a new day. This is the day that the Lord hath made. Let us rejoice and be glad in it. I say that as I get into the shower.

I shave carefully. My hair looks brisk. I dress in clothes that are nice but not too nice, an investment banker or a lawyer on his day off, just a blazer and loafers, and then I have coffee. I make a whole pot, even though I just have a cup and a half. It just looks better. Cozier. Then I wash the cup and the pot and pretty much pace the apartment until ten o'clock. I like to be just a hair late.

The real estate office is a new one, very fancy. They have branches all over the city, but they've just opened a branch here because the neighborhood has gotten hot all over again. It's just gone wild, rents shooting through the roof.

I wait, and then the shower comes out. That's what they call them, the people who show apartments. My shower's name is Chris Mallone. He wears a name plate on his shirt pocket. I almost slip, then tell him my name is Billy Champagne.

He's maybe twenty-nine, not good-looking, just a pasty-faced Irish boy, already going soft around the middle. It's sad to see a person that age look so uncertain in his body. He looks like maybe he drinks too much on a regular basis. He looks like he maybe drank too much just the night before, and stayed out too late. He was probably still out when I woke up to smoke, but he's all smiles, and he's got a good firm handshake, even if his palms are a little sweaty.

Six months from now, Chris Mallone won't be working here anymore. He'll be selling sporting goods at Paragon. Six months after that, he'll be bartending in the East Village, selling double shots at happy hour. He'll move down the food chain so fast and so low he'll be sucking mud off the bottom of the river. And he'll stay there bottom-feeding forever.

It's a shame. He should find his youth a pleasure. He should work out and see a dermatologist. He shouldn't drink so much. There's plenty of time for that later. And if he hates his job, and obviously he hates his job, who wouldn't, he should find something he likes better before the inevitable something worse finds him. It's not too late.

When I was his age, I had a job I loved. It made me feel rich and powerful. Then I just got eaten alive. It was bad at the time, but it's not so bad now.

If you go swimming in a river, and you know there are piranhas in the river, and you get your leg chewed off or something, you can get mad, but you can't get mad at the piranhas. That's what they do.

So, it all changed. I work in a bookshop now. I wear a name plate, like Chris Mallone. But I'm an American and I have health benefits and a 401K and every five years I save up money and go on a vacation to a country where I don't know anybody and don't speak the language. And I go first class. The best of everything, cocktails on the veranda at sunset, a view of the local monument. It reminds me of how it all used to be before it got all fucked up. Without the girls or the drugs or the phone calls.

The apartment I had then was beautiful. This wasn't so long ago, either. It had chic low furniture and the telephone rang all the time and friends dropped over to drink Heineken and leaf through copies of *Details* and *Wallpaper* and talk about whatever it was that was just about to catch the attention of everybody else. Girls with silken skin and sloe eyes spent the night there, and wore my shirts in the morning when they made espresso, in little cups they would bring to me where I lay naked in bed. The girls, who all had great educations and foreign-language skills and mostly trust funds, had fantastic hair and the kind of bodies you see in *Vogue* magazine.

Then the clock stopped ticking. The spring just snapped one day, and the getting stopped and the shocking process of losing began. Not that I have nothing now. I do. I have a lot. You can learn to live with anything. You can do without so much. It's just irredeemably different and I go out looking for some vestige of my old life on the first Tuesday of every month, although I've learned to get along without it, like an amputee who is a marvel because he's adjusted so well.

As Chris goes through the various checkpoints on the form I fill out, I notice that the cuffs of my white shirt are unbuttoned. My mother once said you could always tell a crazy person because they didn't button their cuffs, but I disagree. I think it makes me look like a rock star from the sixties. Like David Bowie in the Thin White Duke days. I've seen pictures.

I think you can tell a crazy person because they always wear too many clothes in the summer and not enough clothes in the winter.

Chris looks eager to help, like he smells blood, although I'm betting he wishes he had a shot of vodka and an Altoid to get him through the next couple of hours.

I tell him exactly what I want. I want a prewar building. I don't need a doorman. I need rooms with architectural details. I'd love a fireplace. I want to move because I've gotten bored with my apartment, it's too bland, although it's nice for what it is. Chris takes notes, then opens a book and begins to shuffle through the listings.

He says he's not sure I can get what I'm looking for at that price. I tell him I'm flexible, that the space is more important than the price, within reason. I'll go to $5,500, if that's what it takes. I tell him I want a place where I can live for a long time.

The thing is, when I'm telling him all these lies, I don't feel fraudulent. I got over that a long time ago.

I feel an almost erotic thrill, deep in my body. I'm wearing hard-soled shoes and a Chesterfield coat with a green velvet collar from Turnbull and Asser that still looks almost as immaculate as it did the day I bought it, before the clock stopped. To Chris, there's no reason to believe I'm not all the things I say I am. This is America, and you can be whoever you want.

The streets are full, the Christmas tree people are already out, have been since Thanksgiving, but mostly they're just standing around in those gloves that don't have any fingers on them, drinking coffee and talking with the Korean flower people. Nobody in town is going to buy a tree the first week of December, but hope is just bleeding through everybody's pores, it would seem.

Chris has a fine film of sweat at his hairline even though the day is brisk despite the bright white sunlight, and he talks on and on about the Knicks and about his girlfriend and about how fast the neighborhood is changing. Meaning getting more expensive, filled with fathers in Barbour coats and horn-rimmed glasses leading their children around to private schools.

The sound of his voice is comforting, and I feel cheerful and ask all the right questions.

I take care to step lightly on the sidewalk. Another thing my mother used to teach us was that a light footfall was a sign of good breeding. I've learned it pretty well, pacing much of the time around my apartment, so the downstairs neighbors won't feel they're living in an Edgar Allan

Poe story. "The Tell-Tale Heart," or something. I expend a great deal of energy trying not to look or seem peculiar.

I've been to Phuket, I want to tell sweating Chris, and China. I've been to Cuba. Stayed at Hotel Nacional. Stayed at the Ritz, in Paris, which makes me the kind of man who stays at the Ritz. I've had more money in my pocket than you have in your bank account most days.

His girlfriend works at the Chanel counter at Saks. She's a makeup artist. I tell him we've never met.

Chris keeps walking toward the first apartment. He's done this yesterday. He did it the day before. As far as Chris is concerned, he's been doing it forever.

We look at seven apartments, except that three are in the same building and two of those are identical, just on different floors. A long time ago, I went to a party in one of these apartments, or one in the same line, as they say.

There is something fatally wrong with every one of them. Well, naturally, there has to be. Like, for instance, one has this peculiar fifties miniature oven, so small you could barely fit a chicken into it. Chris asks me if I cook a lot. Oh yes, I say, I entertain pretty often.

The technique is to make some generally favorable remark when you first walk into at least some of the apartments so that Chris doesn't get too discouraged. And, of course, with the first or second apartment, you have to say,

Chris, this is exactly the apartment I don't want. Just so he knows.

Seeing apartments is essentially a sordid business. Looking at an apartment that the tenant hasn't moved out of yet makes me really squeamish.

One time, I looked at this nice apartment, prewar, doorman, nice, and the tenant hadn't moved out and when I opened the bedroom closets there were all his clothes hanging there and I realized the tenant was a midget. Boy, that was weird, and I imagined myself living this kind of miniature life, never forgetting the deformed little suits, the tiny shoes, always feeling like Alice after she's gotten really big.

I couldn't get out of there fast enough, and it was rent-stabilized and had a working fireplace.

You spend about ten minutes in each apartment, each redolent with lives lived totally unaware of your own, each filled with the promise of an imaginary life you might live there, where your clothes would go in the closets, where you would put the sofa and the television, and how loud it would be from the street.

I always imagine, right off, where I would put the Christmas tree. I know it's trivial; it's two weeks of the year and, besides, I haven't had a tree for years, not a full-sized one, just a little table-topper, as tacky people say, but I don't know what else you call it when it sits on a table and isn't even a tree, really.

But I try to find a spot and picture a majestic eight-footer, covered with all the extravagant ornaments I've saved from my old life, the days when everything glittered too brightly.

Somewhere in these lonely rooms there is the ghost of the life I might have there. Somewhere there is room for a wife and two or three children and a Sussex spaniel and Barbour jackets and travel tickets lying on the kitchen table.

In that lovely room I see her. Her hair is colored once a month by the best colorist in the city, tawny blonde with highlights. She's a partner at Debevoise & Plimpton and she never cooks so we eat out all the time, or order in, and the three children are in private school, the youngest girl at Spence, the boy at Collegiate, the elder girl at Foxcroft where we let her go because of her equestrian passions, and, face it, she's not ever going to be a Rhodes scholar. Every morning, I kiss them and go off to McCann-Erickson where I am a global creative director, working on some of their biggest accounts. I am pivotal. I am rewarded beyond the common imagination.

I see her in another apartment, I see her. She looks sort of like Barbra Streisand at the end of *The Way We Were,* and she works as head of one of the departments at the library and I work at a small publishing house and we are very left-ist and the children go to the Little Red Schoolhouse and then on to Horace Mann when they get older. We only have two children. Our hearts would hold a dozen, but that's all we could afford. We use our MetroCards all the time, and we take a subscription in the Family Circle at the Met and the children will grow up to lead lives intense with intelligent ideas and passionate views and commitments.

Every apartment grows other rooms, grows organically into a place where a family could live for years and years.

And, in every apartment, there is always a Christmas tree. It's all covered with beautiful ornaments, Bavarian glass, that we have collected over the years and put away with care and never broken any of, except that one time the tree fell over, all mixed in with funny kids' stuff and a tree topper made out of rhinestones and popsicle sticks that Kate made when she was six and which now fills her with both uncertain pride and mortification every time we take it out and put it right at the very tippy-top.

In one life, the Plimpton/McCann life, we give each other extravagant fur and remote-controlled things and bijoux and bibelots, and we leave Christmas afternoon to go skiing in Europe for a week, because the airports are empty on Christmas Day.

In the library life, we share mittens and scarves and *Letters of Leonard Woolf* and baskets made in Third World countries and then we eat a big dinner in the middle of the afternoon and then we go for a walk in the snowy, almost deserted streets.

In one life, we are giddy but anxious. In the other, we are happy. Just a happy family.

In another apartment, I live with a woman. She is tall, with the long, lean body of a swimmer. She is ten years younger than I am, and she wears designer clothes and shoes that cost a month's salary for most people. She is a graphic designer and the apartment is a monument to good taste. We are wholly happy in ourselves, and we have no children. I am a writer. I write novels that make people feel better about themselves, and they sell quite well. You'd know me if you saw me, from the dust jackets.

We entertain a lot—actresses, publishers, people from the arts—and we discuss Tristan Tzara and the Dadaists and Le Désert de Retz around coq au vin and Muscadet.

She once wrote to me from Paris, "You are to me as water to a man dying of thirst in the desert."

In any case, every case, we are a tribe, a law unto ourselves, filled with quirks that have come to seem perfectly natural to us. We have the pride of knowing that there is no other group of people in the world with our unique qualities of beauty and intelligence, or kindness or grace or strength. We are only wholly ourselves when we are together. Each completes a part of the whole.

But the apartments I look at today couldn't hold any of this. They could hold only me, and I feel bereft each time a door closes behind us.

On West Twelfth Street, we meet another broker with her client at a double brownstone. The apartment is composed of the back half of the ground floor and the first floor, what used to be called the parlor floor.

The other client is English, in his early thirties, and we all go in together and look at this peculiar apartment. He is eating a green apple.

We go in to the space, as city dwellers say these days, the space. The ground floor is peculiarly divided into two small rooms, one a kind of office, I guess, and the other the dining room, which looks out into a large, wintry garden filled with Italian terra-cotta urns. Then there is a handsome galley kitchen with its own washer/dryer combination. The ceilings are low and the rooms are dark.

There is a treacherous cantilevered staircase jerryrigged to get up to the second floor, which is perfectly wonderful.

There is a ballroom-size sitting room with fourteen-foot ceilings. You could have a twelve-footer in here, easy. There is simple but elegant plaster molding. The windows look out onto the garden, and would be just at leaf level in the spring and summer.

Behind this there is a large bedroom, which is closed off from the living room by elegant sliding etched-glass doors, and an art deco bathroom with a real deep cast-iron tub. It is all magnificent.

I am trembling with excitement. You can feel the weight of the lives lived in these rooms. It has an upstairs and a downstairs, like a real house. Once the whole brownstone was home to a single family, now it is carved up into separate spaces, disparate lives. You can almost hear the rustle of their skirts as the other agent slides the glass doors back and forth.

The other realtor turns to her young English client. "But where would you put the baby?" She asks, and he says exactly and they leave right away.

I want to stay there, listening to the sounds of my wife and children, watching the tree glisten in the early winter afternoon, but my ten minutes are almost up, and I don't want Chris to get overstimulated or he'll never leave me alone.

But I can see them. I can smell them. I can lie down in the bedroom, rich or poor, and sink into the comfort of twenty years of marriage to a woman I love. I can see the posters of the rock stars and the sports heroes on the walls of my children's bedrooms.

I'm not a fantasist. I know the place where I really live. The one room is comfortable to me, and it isn't so bad. It is dark and it is small but it's also pretty much free from memory. There's a lot you can do with a one-room apartment if you use your imagination.

I know what I do and where I am in the world, which is pretty far down the *People* magazine Most Beautiful People ladder.

But I want things. The things I had in another life. I'm sorry I threw it all away. I feel terrible about fucking it all up, all the time. I want to tell Chris all this, I always do, but I don't say anything. I just take another tour through the rooms, remarking mostly on how they cut these brownstones up in such peculiar ways, and then we leave.

I look again at the twinkling tree, so brief, so fragile. I look through the tall windows into the garden where I might barbecue for friends on a summer night, white wine and chevre. Diana Krall. The *New York Review of Books.*

I kiss my wife good-bye. I kiss my loving children on their foreheads and Chris and I go back out into the fading sunlight. It's really cold now.

This apartment costs $6,000 a month, more than three times what I'm paying now.

On the way back to the office, I tell Chris that his job must be very frustrating, showing all these apartments to people who are so hard to satisfy. He says that it's OK, he likes people. He says he has one client who's been looking for an apartment for five months. He says he just takes it one day at a time.

That's the way you ought to take it, pal, I think. One day at a time.

I shake his hand, promise I'll call him tomorrow. I walk home through the chill afternoon, passing the tree stand again. Maybe this year, I think. Maybe next week.

The windows we look through to glimpse the happiness of families.

All the rooms we might have lived in. All the lives we might have led.

CHAPTER SIX

One Reason I Don't Go
to the Beach Anymore

❖　❖　❖

More than a decade ago, a lifetime ago, really, I rented a lovely summer house by the sea. Not exactly by the sea, but close enough, and it had a big pool and five bedrooms and a sunroom and an English box garden and you could see the ocean from a widow's walk on the roof. It was owned by these two interior decorators so everything was just so and it was all kind of perfectly done in an English-country-house kind of way and filled with light and shadow. It was everything my apartment in town wasn't and it was just swell.

It was like being in an episode of *Masterpiece Theater*. All you needed was an under housemaid arranging flowers in cut glass vases.

This was just as the great tailgate party was coming to an end, and I had an almost infinite amount of money. Or so it seemed.

I worked on The Street, and while I didn't particularly enjoy helping rich people shift money around every minute of every day so that they could get even richer at the expense of people who had no money and never would have—I was wracked with guilt at the same time I was insane with adrenaline and raging testosterone—still, the money was fantastic and the roll, the flow of it, was like mainlining every day. The roll smelled like money. You could feel the poison boiling through your veins. Money was the big news, the lifeblood of the decade, and I was in it up to my elbows.

I worked in a big room that was basically like a casino; there were no windows, no clocks, nothing but the relentless flicker of financial news on dozens of TV sets. It was both timeless and relentless. The days were vicious, but the nights were filled with fat stogies in the cigar room at Frank's and big steaks and then on to clubs where we swaggered in our monogrammed Sea Island cotton shirts and $200 scarf ties from Hermès and sat in the VIP section and ran up $2,000 bar bills and took town cars home at three in the morning when we had to be back at the office at seven-thirty. We did things like write our phone numbers on girls' tits with Mont Blanc pens, and they always called us back. Always.

You could smoke then, that's how long ago it was.

This was life. This was everyday life, and we didn't understand people who didn't live like this. We were the pulse, the heartbeat, of the decade and we were all young and mostly good looking and we all found time to work out like dogs, weird times like six in the morning, so we had these fantastic bodies, well, not all of us had fantastic bodies, some had the spindly hollow-eyed stares of junkies and some topped three hundred pounds and smoked three packs of cigarettes a day; but I'm thinking about the guys who came to the house that summer, we were all in perfect shape and had the kind of women you get when you have a fantastic body and a wad of cash and the utter arrogance that comes with having the big dog on the leash.

We were the people people wrote about when they wrote about the evils of contemporary society. We made too much money. We spent too much money. We didn't do a single thing to help the less fortunate, which included most of the people on the planet. We drank too much. We did too many drugs. We had eighteen-year-old kids with rasta braids coming to drop shit off in the middle of the day. We went to Alphabet City the minute we got into our black town cars at the end of a stressful day. We felt not one ounce of remorse. We only felt pity for the rest of the gray masses. All of these things were true. But, man, did we have fun. It was like a giant testosterone flambé.

Bonuses were a big thing. Bonuses were given out around Christmastime, in yards, a yard being a million dollars. People would say, sucking on a big fat Cubano, that they got a yard or a yard and a half. Everybody lied, of course, but everybody got a lot and it was a big deal.

I wasn't necessarily the brightest nickel in the bag, but I had the best education, and I was as aggressive as a pit bull, I could trade shit for silk, and so I was good for half a yard at least. I was thirty-one.

After I paid off the taxes and my enormous bills—I owed Bergdorf's $12,000, which was basically three suits, two cashmere sweaters, and a bottle of Acqua di Parma, the same cologne Cary Grant wore—I still had quite a pile, and I decided to get my own house in the Hamptons. Not just any house, *the* house.

I had shared before. Little bungalows on Gin Lane. I had gone through the ritual of being a houseguest—my mother once said, when you're a houseguest, don't ring the doorbell with anything but your elbow, so I took cases of champagne and new badminton sets from Hammacher Schlemmer—so I knew what I wanted was a palace of my own, where I could invite people every weekend, and have them bring me lavish and largely unusable stuff.

I looked at six houses. I took the sixth one. It was chintzed and striped and leopard-printed, stuff that would charm women, and it had a grand piano and a deck from which you could smell the sea, and the pool and the garden and service for thirty. It was English aristocracy without the dog shit and the cigarette burns in the upholstery.

Someone witty once said to me that living in a castle wasn't all it was cracked up to be. "Darling," she said, "you still have to wash your hair in the bathtub."

I had never been in an English country house. I thought this was the real thing. I rented it immediately. It cost $96,000, Memorial Day to Labor Day, and I wrote a check. The house came with a maid, so the owners could feel safe about their fabulous stuff, and she cost another $800 a week, which I also paid by check, and I leased a car for the summer, a deeply impressive convertible Mercedes, midnight black, with every accoutrement you could wish for and the smell of brand-new leather and a top that slid back with the touch of a button, slid back as silently as a snake through the grass. This was a very nice car. I gave them my platinum card.

I bought sheets in the city for every bedroom, from Frette, since the sheets that were there were the kind of clever pastiche designed to make you think maybe Kmart was a good idea after all. My guests would sleep in thousand-thread-count cotton, white with scalloped borders, so the cool night air could pass over their bodies like a lover's kiss.

I still have the sheets. Quality lasts.

I found a huge Moroccan tent in the city and bought it for $25,000 and had it put up on the lawn and filled with benches and silk pillows and those low kind of Moroccan tables and hung with chandeliers so it was like being in a fantasy seraglio, all about sex. It was hot as hell in there, like being at a rinky-dink circus on a July afternoon in Reno, Nevada, but it was lavishly and painstakingly embroidered and dotted with thousands of tiny little mirrors and it was breathtakingly beautiful.

From the second story of the house, you looked down at the roof of it, or whatever tents have, and it was like looking down at the stars, with all the mirrors twinkling and the candles glowing softly through the canvas.

The first weekend, I invited my main buddies from The Firm—George, who was hysterical, and Frank, who was enormous, 6'4", just to show I wasn't filled with self-doubt, and Fanelli and Trotmeier. I took two days off from work to stock the house, bread and desserts from the Barefoot Contessa, $30-a-pound lobster salad from Loaves and Fishes, and all kinds of salads and hors d'oeuvres and candy and cakes from all over and vegetables from the Green Thumb. And liquor, Jesus. Everything you could imagine. I even stopped by the road and bought tall flowers to go in all those vases, and little bunches in every room, and when

I was done the whole thing looked like an at-home *Vogue* shoot showing how some English heiress lived when she was tired of town and longed for the simple life.

Friday night, they all showed up, with the girls, and I picked Carmela up from the Jitney and we were a household. The girls, frankly, were the least of it. Everybody assumed they would be beautiful and pliable and enviable and basically disposable. So, all summer, the house was the five guys and whatever the cat dragged in.

And the presents. Like Christmas all over again. George brought a case of 1966 Romanee-Conti Montrachet, God knows where he found it, and Frank brought a picnic hamper from Bergdorf's with real china plates, and Fanelli, who was a thug, brought a Z of really good coke, and Trotmeier brought ten white beach towels with my initials on them, every monogram a different color.

We drank rum drinks that came out of a blender. Frank claimed he'd never seen a blender before and Trotmeier said he'd never tasted rum. His mother told him it was the devil's drink and taught him never to touch it. He got over that pretty fast, and Frank became a whizmaster at making blended drinks because he was mechanically inclined, he said.

The household was perfect. It was a complete universe, all by itself. We ate butterflied leg of lamb on the Weber grill, and we drank rum and Montrachet until we were silly and did many, many lines of fine white cocaine, but only after we'd eaten the lamb with this $90-a-bottle Burgundy I had laid in, and we smoked Cuban cigars until the whole angst of the week had worn away, and we went to bed at two in the morning to sleep with these beautiful girls and the sex was not quiet and every form of human sensuality was redolent in the quiet night air.

The next morning by eleven, everybody was fresh as a daisy. Juices were poured, omelets got made and eaten out on the sunporch, and then Bloody Marys got made and drunk out by the pool, and then the guys went off to play tennis. We knew this one guy, a yard and a half at least, who had hired a tennis pro for the summer to come every Saturday afternoon, so we got to going over there, knocking balls around while the women looked on and read novels, us quick-footed in our $300 Prada tennis shorts and our raggedy old T-shirts from Joe's Stone Crab in Miami, Florida, and places like that, just to show we weren't fashion pussies.

We were the kind of people who got their pictures in *Hamptons* magazine. We were the kind of people who dressed in Nantucket-red linen trousers to go to the Hampton Classic Horse Show. We could get into Nick and Toni's—impossible to get into—on thirty minutes' notice. That kind of people.

The second weekend, we really found the perfect thing to round out the house. We found a pet.

Her name was Giulia de Bosset. She was European. I found her at a party.

She came up to me at the bar while I was getting more drinks for everybody and she looked straight at me and said, "I know *you*." As though we were in the middle of some conversation already.

"I'm sorry. I don't . . . what?"

"I know *you*. I met you when you were still at Hopkins. I was just a little girl."

It turned out she was the baby sister of the college roommate of this extremely thin girl I used to date—we called her the Pencil—and so we rehashed old times, and I asked her where she was staying and she said she was staying at the God-forsaken Maidstone Club, of all places, her father was a member, as was his father and grandfather, with all those old farts, so I told her to come stay with us, where at least she could get some peace and quiet without somebody whacking golf balls all over the place. Things were different then. We spit at golf.

So she came. We picked up her things at two in the morning, and she came and slept in the little maid's room off the kitchen, which she said was just fine with her, anywhere but that mausoleum.

She was a waif. She was like Audrey Hepburn, not that I knew who Audrey Hepburn was at the time. That was just one piece of information that hadn't been downloaded yet.

Later, I kept hearing her name, especially when she died, so I went and rented all these old movies and boy, she was something, and boy, was she ever like Giulia de Bosset. I bet neither one of them ever went to a dance where they had to get their hands stamped if they wanted to get back in.

Giulia was naïve and quiet and had chopped-off hair and lived in the East Village where nobody lived in those days, and she would tell funny stories about finding guys shooting up on her stairs, and she talked about getting mugged by those same guys and she obviously had money and we were all intrigued and we just adored her and so we asked her back. And she came.

She came every weekend, and slept in the little maid's room off the kitchen. I went back to Frette and got sheets for her, too, so she wouldn't feel bad about staying in the single bed in the little room that barely had a bathroom. Her sheets were very fancy, embroidered with vines in periwinkle blue, so her room would seem special in some way.

She wasn't as pretty as the other girls. She wasn't athletic. She didn't like to lie in the sun. But she was slim as a reed and had flawless skin and boy, could she make a great Greek salad. Give her a lemon, some really good olive oil, some mustard, some garlic, and some kosher sea salt, and she could really make a salad into a whole new thing. It took her a long time to do it, but it was worth every second.

She had no interest in sex, and believe me, we tried. Even Trotmeier tried, and he was very fastidious.

She said she was a virgin and she had a kind of quietude as though she weren't even waiting for something and anything that happened was just fine with her.

She'd show up every weekend. We offered to drive her but she said she liked the jitney, she liked getting the free water and looking at all the faces not looking at one another, and she'd show up at sunset with an overstuffed vintage Vuitton satchel, and out of that bag would come the most fantastic clothes, some all spangled and beaded, some the kind you'd wear to the Queen's garden party, not that we knew what you'd actually wear to such an event, but you get the picture. She had the right outfit for anything we went to, and she looked just fantastic lying in the seraglio in the afternoon in jeans and a T-shirt, reading Jane Austen.

She apparently disdained water sports. We never saw her in a bathing suit.

She was a smackhead, of course. You could tell that right away. All those European kids were, then. But she never did it in public. She never shared. She would just get all winsome and content and dozy and you could tell. We never asked her. She never did cocaine with us after dinner, just sipped her white wine and looked far, far into the future. She was probably twenty-three, so there was a lot of future to look into.

The women liked her because she posed no threat whatsoever to anybody, and the men liked her because she was like a little parakeet with beautiful plumage you could have sit on the tip of your index finger and just stare at it, just for the pleasure of the colors and the loveliness of life beating in her little chest.

We called her Jools and, like any good pet, she came when she was called and, like some pets, you could possess her for a while, but she let you know you could never really own her, not really. Like a cat. Like a fish. Like a bird on your finger.

She had a sweetly vague Continental accent, unlike most of the girls who hung around that summer, and she actually had a job. Not that she got paid. In fact, she paid to do it.

She was in New York for the summer studying art restoration with this tiny little man on Greene Street, the ogre, she called him, and together they were working on restoring the largest Titian in the world still in private hands. She seemed to know a lot about art. The rest of us, in general, knew nothing about art, beyond your basic Art History 101 kind of stuff, although we went to galleries like Castelli and

Mary Boone and spent enormous sums on the latest and coolest decorations, now mostly in warehouses, I assume. Mine are long gone, I know that. Ten cents on the dollar.

The funny thing is, I can't remember one witty thing she said all summer. She wasn't funny or clever in that way. Not one remark. She never even tried, just stared at you with her calm and tender expressions and smiled like La Gioconda at something only she knew about. She didn't fit in, of course. Maybe that was part of the charm.

She could play the piano, anything from Bach to "Hey Jude," and some nights when we weren't too wrecked, or came home early from a boring party, she'd play for us and we'd stand around the piano singing. Most of us were terrible, except for Fanelli, who had a real sweetness in his voice, a clarity and kindness that embarrassed even him, but, if you could get him to sing, you went to bed feeling life was a pretty good thing, after all.

I know we all wondered what she did, lying there in the nights listening to the howling storms of sex all around her, smelling the smells, feeling the vibrations, lying in her virginal bed in her immaculate sheets. She probably just nodded off, nodded out, but she must have been aware. It was what the house was about, all those rutting nights, and she must have been aware.

But she'd appear at breakfast in time to do all the dishes,

and she never complained about the slightest thing, and there was a serenity about her that defied any but pharmaceutical explanations.

The maid came every day during the week, so the house was immaculate every weekend, but Jools made sure we left it the way we found it. We never broke a single thing that whole summer. Not a glass.

Even when we had forty people over to grill tenderloins and drink champagne, even when we went to bed as the sun was coming up, Jools kept up her relentless tidying, kind of somewhere between a guest and a caterer, so that if things went bad on either end, she could hop to the other side and stay out of trouble. We adored her.

She said dishes had to be washed and dried by hand. She said dishwashers left a film of soap on everything and that wasn't kind to the next guest. She loved doing dishes, and we stood around her like puppies, drying them and putting them away, while the women smoked and glared. Dishwashing time took away from drinking champagne and doing coke, and they tapped their feet impatiently until the last dish was put away.

And then one weekend she died. Hummingbirds' hearts beat so fast that, if they stop to rest or sleep, their hearts slow down and sometimes they can't get them to get up to speed again, so they die without ever waking up.

I found her.

She didn't show up for breakfast, which wasn't unusual, and she missed the narcissistic hour by the pool and the tennis that she never went to anyway, and when we came home we assumed she'd gone to the beach or for a walk, or just didn't feel like it that Saturday.

It wasn't until the Waring blender had started up that we thought to look in her room. I knocked softly, a little harder, and then turned the handle.

She was lying in her perfect sheets, and there was blood coming from her nose and her mouth. There was vomit on her ruined silk nightgown.

By her hand, there were open glassine envelopes of heroin, with powder spilling on to the sheets. By the bed, on the nightstand, there was an empty bottle of Seconal. There was no note.

I didn't know what to do. I didn't cry. I didn't call out. I just watched her, the soft lids closed over her azure eyes.

I took a cloth and cleaned the blood from her face. I used warm water, knowing it wouldn't make any difference to Giulia. Her skin was so cold, and, underneath the blood, she was as sweet and unfazed as ever. Even death hadn't surprised her.

I touched her face. I kissed her icy cheek. It was the only time I had ever touched her.

Then I went into the kitchen and told the others. The

blender stopped. We agreed to clean the house of any drugs before we called 911, so each of us went to our rooms and brought down whatever we had.

We put it all in a big trash bag, and Fanelli drove it down to Sagg Main Beach and buried it in the sand, with an old tire over the spot so we could go back and get it.

Then we made the call. They came in seconds. The rest is a blur. The rest is just the same details as anybody else's death.

There were questions, of course. There was a search of the house. Everything was in order.

We let the barbecue burn out, while we sat and drank hard liquor. We went out to dinner and ate in silence.

Then we drove back to the beach at midnight to retrieve the drugs. Funny thing, a lot of people didn't want to claim what was theirs. We sat there with a counter full of drugs that seemed to have no owners.

Fanelli sang a quiet, tiny song. It was in Italian. Then I sat up very late and got very drunk and did drugs all by myself until the sky was blue.

That was the first weekend in August. It happened on my birthday.

I went to the funeral. We all went. Turned out, her father was a French count who was tiny and ugly. He had a gigantic art collection, one of the most important in the world. Museums were already fighting over it.

Her mother was dead, but her stepmother was a Spanish knockout who had been an airline stewardess. I didn't speak to them.

The coffin was open. She was perfect, calm and lovely, in a simple, embroidered-cotton nightgown. She was a countess, and she was finally the prettiest girl in the room. *La Serenissima.*

You say to yourself, she wasn't the kind, she wasn't the kind to do that. But there was the empty bottle of Seconal. She knew what she was doing. It was time for her to leave the party where she never really met anybody, for though many asked her to dance, there was no Prince Charming.

There was an article about it in the weekly rag, the death of a countess kind of article, a here's what happens to careless international trash in the Hamptons kind of article, and that's how I know that part about the airline stewardess thing. Apparently she was a big deal back in France. She was, according to the article, the kind of girl who knew that tiaras weren't just pinned on your head, they were woven into your hair. It took hours, and it hurt like hell. She was the kind of girl who was going to marry a king, if one could be found.

She was just slumming, with us. She was just trying not to be who she was for a little while. Drinking cold Montrachet, dreaming, with Jane Austen open on her lap, in a Moroccan tent, and removing tiny smudges of grime from a Titian that happened to belong to her father.

I refused to talk to the reporters. I said I didn't know who she was, and couldn't tell them a thing about her. I couldn't tell them about the blood on her face or the vomit on her silk nightgown.

We had three weeks left in the house, and we drank blender drinks and lay in the seraglio in the cool evenings and drank cold Dom Perignon and did cocaine and laughed and had people over for barbecues, but it was never the same. I was drunk every minute of every day. All weekend, every weekend. Even Fanelli was drunk and sad all the time. It wasn't creepy, but the bubble had gone out of the champagne.

We skipped the last weekend, Labor Day. We got there Friday night and left Saturday morning. We just didn't feel like it.

I left the tent where it was. Let somebody else deal with it. The summer had cost me almost $200,000.

Three months later I was in rehab. Again. This time for the last time.

One day I came back from lunch, three martinis and big slabs of rare beef and raw cocaine under my belt, and I stood and waited for the elevator. The doors opened, and a voice very clearly said to me. "Don't get on to that elevator. If you do, you will die." The doors closed, all the happy bees going back to the hive, and I went home.

They were very understanding. The personnel woman

called me, and I hadn't bathed or shaved in six days and I broke down on the phone, blubbered like a baby about my lost, lost ways, and she offered to have me sent to rehab, and I packed up my sweats and went, leaving twenty-eight days later so clean and sober it hurt, and filled with boredom and self-loathing.

Then they fired me. I never even went back to get my last check.

Once you leave The Street, you don't go back, not even to buy a hot dog from the Sabbrett's man on the corner. And then the phone rings less and less and eventually Fanelli was the last one to call to say one more time how sorry he was and what a great summer it had been, except for, well, you know, the Thing, and that we really would get together one of these days. My brilliant suits hung in the closets like lost quotations. Like yellowed maps of another world and time.

And I never went and wrote my phone number on a girl's tits again. Little by little you lose it all, until you're left with the pure electric shock of the sober life. A life without friends, without money, without trainers at the gym, without countesses who die while under your watch. And nobody ever called me Billy Champagne again.

Six months later, I was broke. Nine months later, I was selling running shoes at Paragon.

I worked a series of jobs. I started drinking again. But

never in public. The trouble with drinking in public is (1) the glasses aren't big enough; (2) somebody uglier and drunker than you is always hitting on you; and (3) there's no place to lie down.

The other night, I was coming back from the bookstore where I eventually ended up working. Now I'm the supervisor of the ordinary clerks, and the two girls at the checkout counter were talking and one was showing off her new bracelet to the other girl, and she said, "Girl, I mean, ain't this bracelet *bad*? Like ain't it just soooo *bad*!"

And the other girl, bagging my pork chops and broccoli, said, "Girl, it's so bad it's *fatal*."

Well, it's all fatal, isn't it, in the end?

I look at my Christmas tree. It's kind of short and scrawny, the way my life is lived now. It suits me. But the ornaments are miraculous, collected over the years when I got a yard and a half two weeks before Christmas, boats, and tigers and Buddhas and Santas and Satin and ruby slippers. Mouth-blown in Czechoslovakia, when there was one. Dozens of them, thousand of dollars. The ornaments are all the girls who came that summer, the mirrors on the tent, the grams of coke.

Almost every night, when I'm lying in bed, I hear an ornament fall and break. They break because there are no presents under the tree to cushion the fall, only bare wood floor. I come home from work, and there is shattered glass everywhere, every day. My ornamented life is fading, and I don't really miss it.

Until the swan. This morning, Christmas morning, a beautiful pearl-white swan had fallen and was shattered on the floor. I hadn't even heard it fall in the night, and I knew it was Giulia. The image of her, so swanlike, came back to me as clear as crystal. The sound of her voice. The sweet smell of her nightgown in the morning. The Titian and her stewardess wicked stepmother, also dead now, the shining Titian, now in the Prado in Madrid.

Like the swan, Jools was an ornament in a life I no longer have and don't miss. But, as I swept up the pieces, she cried out to me not to go, not to be thrown away. Not to lie in pieces in the garbage with the rest of the detritus of my life. And, one more time, I couldn't help her.

I just couldn't help her.

CHAPTER SEVEN

Carmela in the Flats at Thirty-One

❖ ❖ ❖

In those days, we were vampires for parties. We would search out the Scene, whatever the Scene of the moment happened to be, and we would suck it dry and leave it for suburbanites and out-of-towners. We would go anywhere for a party. We were bicoastal, transcontinental. Especially for Carmela's birthday, which was an event equivalent to the Easter Octave in the Holy City.

Did I tell you we got married? We did. It was sort of an accident. It actually wasn't so much like a marriage as it was like a long, drunken date. Her great-great-grandfather, Alexandre, had started a French, now international, banking house in 1848 with $9,000 in his pocket, and she was *set,* baby, and a killer on The Street and a total whore in bed. She was one of the boys. We got married at their place in East Hampton one June afternoon, in a tent that seated four hundred with a dinner catered by Glorious Foods. She had only peonies for decoration, these huge arrangements. She actually bought the entire crop of peonies that came into New York that year, drove the price through the roof, and our wedding present was our own house on West End Road in East Hampton. Best present I ever got, I have to admit. Five bedrooms.

Valentino made her dress. It involved three trips to Europe on the Concorde, Carmela and her mother, a suite at the Hassler, and then the thing came in a box you could barely have squeezed a suit into. He made an extra skirt, in black, so that, if things went south, she could wear it again. She was an hour late for the wedding.

She told me, years later, just before the slamming door, that, as she sat there in her hair and makeup and dress, her mother at the bottom of the landing calling out, the guests in the church itching for a cocktail, she looked at her face in the mirror and she suddenly knew. She was making the worst mistake of her life. And she was paralyzed with nausea at the thought of marrying me. Me.

That was yet to come, that part. Along with all the rest. At the moment, we had chased Carmela's birthday to

Beverly Hills, where her dear friends Delia and Buzzy gave her a party that was sort of like a second wedding reception. We were poolside at the Beverly Wilshire Hotel in Beverly Hills, California. We had picked the Wilshire because Dino, the indomitable maître d' at the Beverly Hills Hotel had died, presumably now handing out the best tables in Heaven to those lucky few with the fame or the grease to get one. "Always go for a banquette," Carmela said. "I grew up on banquettes."

I had personally attended Dino's funeral a few years before and had watched as the bleary-eyed mourners dropped centuries into the grave as the coffin was lowered. They did this to secure, with one final pourboire, a corner banquette with a telephone in Heaven's Polo Lounge, assuming traffic wasn't overly heavy that week.

So, Dino dead, we had moved on to the Wilshire, because the Bel Air was dull as toast points, and because Carmela longed to walk the carpeted halls where Barbara Hutton had hobbled out her final days and others, many others, had merely played and moved on. She also liked the idea that, somewhere in the hotel, on some high floor, somebody's ceiling was Warren Beatty's floor. She had enormous empathy for his room-service kind of life. At the pool at the Beverly Wilshire, they paged him by number, not by name. He was number three.

In hotels, every night, Carmela dreamt always and only of the people who had stayed in the room the night before. Once, she dreamt a woman had lost a diamond bracelet from Van Cleef & Arpels beneath the bed and in the morning she looked under the bed and there it was. And she kept it. Once, it was a fur coat in a closet, but the closet was empty that time. Mostly it was sexual couplings I would never have imagined without pictures of naked people from India.

Poolside, she turned to me. "I wish you were dead."

She meant it, too. The night before, in the flats, at Delia and Buzzy's on Rexford Drive, I had wrecked Carmela's thirty-first birthday. I had not been, I was informed on the way home, sufficiently festive. Memory poolside is vague, but I seemed to recall having made a spectacle, having insulted a roomful of nearly beautiful people. Perhaps it wasn't quite a full room by the time I got to the spectacle part but I had put on quite a show.

"Oh, God. Now I remember it all."

"Damn, you, Rooney, how could you have done it? And where the hell is my Bloody Mary?" She whistled through her fingers like she was hailing a cab on Park at five thirty, in the rain, and a pool boy approached, silent in his Tretorns, his golden thighs slick with oil and youth, swishing as though he were wearing real silk stockings.

Drinks orders were apparently not his station, he *folded*

the towels, but he snapped his fingers for a charming but seemingly alingual Argentinian whose language skills extended only so far as the names of cocktails, but who only had to look in Carmela's eyes to know what was on her mind.

"I mean, my dearest, my darling, how could you have done it?"

" 'The sedge has withered from the lake, and no birds sing,' " I said.

"Leave Keats out of this," she snapped.

"I don't know. Because I hate flying Flight Number One F class to Los Angeles to take meetings. Because I hated myself for running up and down Rodeo like a lunatic looking for the perfect something and finding nothing except this one thing that matters a lot to me, a lot a lot, only to have you toss my present on the table and say, 'How nice.' I hate eating at Mr Chow's with Helen Reddy at the next table. I hate sitting in the El Padrino room in this hotel, having, no, *buying* drinks for people who think they're so cool because they have composed the masterpieces of our age, all of which can be seen and heard in thirty seconds on the Superbowl. Their complete works can be viewed in less time than it takes to smoke a cigarette.

"But most of all, my darling Carmela, it's because I hate your birthday."

Luckily, the Argentinian appeared with our drinks,

doubles, for both, and we both leapt forward like rats in an alley. From the first sip, as I lay back into a blessed forever of vodka, it was clear to me that somebody had put epoxy on my eyelids. They would never open again.

Carmela, with that infinite and luminous sadness that was one of her finest tropes, said to me, her voicing barely piercing the infinite darkness in which I would happily lie forever, "Let's start this again. You're overwrought. The meetings you took did not go well. The cocaine was cut with angel dust or French bread crumbs for all I know. You lost fifteen thousand dollars at Santa Anita. The Santa Ana is blowing. Some malevolent something."

"With the deepest regrets, and profound apologies, I'll stick. I hate your birthday."

"It was a sweet present. A book, wasn't it? Thoughtful. If I read, I would probably read it." Carmela said. "You have nothing to regret. In that department."

From the weight, I could tell someone had sat down on the end of my chaise. I didn't even have to open my eyes. "Margot, you incorrigible lesbian," I said. "I've been drunk in Los Angel*eeees* for four days. Give a dying man your hand."

"Poor baby," she said. "You poor little dollycakes. Why is Carmela crying? And how does she do it? Jesus, her tears are actually tear-shaped. Perfectly formed little crystal tears."

"Thanks for the silk blouse, Margot. It's divine," said Carmela.

"Oh, just a little something."

"That little something cost $285 at Saint-Germaine," I said. "I happen to know. I ran into Margot there with some ravishing truck-stop worker, or so she appeared."

"Well, we can't walk around nekkid," said Margot. "Anyway, I'll put it on my expense report." Margot had one of those professions that caused people frequently to ask her what she *really* did once she told them what she actually did do. This work did give her the benefit of a seemingly endless expense account that could keep her in the Beverly Wilshire for months at a time. She did not stay in the old wing, second floor, lanai side, possibly because she preferred the clinical anonymity of the *moderne* fifth floor of the new wing, where the rooms somehow resembled a bathysphere Jacques Cousteau might have used to explore marine life at depths to which I was quickly becoming acquainted. Square bathtubs. Foil wallpaper. Ghastly.

"At the risk of repeating myself, I'll ask again. Why is Carmela crying?"

"I ruined her birthday party."

"It's true," said Carmela. "He ruined it. We're dead as doornails in this town. We could stay here for the rest of our lives and nobody would send so much as a pot of ranunculus to our room."

"Ranunculus is the oldest cultivated flower in the world."

"Rooney, you are a master of the timed digression. I have a heavy date at two and don't have time for these horticultural interludes. Why did you ruin her birthday party?"

"Because I hate her birthday."

"Lord, everybody hates her birthday. What I'm interested in, since I attended this fête, is what exactly caused this ruination?"

"I will see you both in hell for this," said Carmela, taking another Bloody from the all-knowing Argentinian. "I'll ask God to make your bones hurt at an early age."

"My bones hurt now," I said. "And it's so dark."

"At least He doesn't hate my birthday."

"*He* doesn't have to go to it," said Margot. "Now come on kiddies, the meter is running." She slid a fresh drink into my hand with the deft skill of those who nurse the difficult and the ill.

"I insulted everybody," I said.

"You didn't insult me."

"You had gone off to go slam dancing with the truck-stop diva. It was after all of that. It started when I told Vilmos Zsigmond that he didn't know the first thing about depth of field. Not to mention Laszlo Kovacs, the master, who was standing nearby. I told them I would send them all a copy of the *American Cinematographer Manual*. I used a specific gesture, a gesture it now nauseates me to remember, to indicate the difference between near and far. Then I broke several things."

"Every word is true," said Carmela. "He hates my birthday."

"This sounds so much better than a roomful of women in flannel shirts banging into one another," said Margot. "I'm sorry I left. Rooney, why did you do this disgusting stuff?"

"Because she threw my present on the floor. And then she laughed. And then everybody laughed. Laughed at me."

"Well, it was a scummy present. A paperback book? In Beverly Hills?"

"It was a very good paperback book. It contained one line that summed up Carmela in her entirety: 'Let's take the river road down to the casino. It takes longer, but nothing ever happens before ten anyway.' Michael Arlen Jr.'s mother said that as she lay dying."

"I even wrote it in the front of the book, so she wouldn't have to read the whole thing. She could just read the inscription and the 'Love, Rooney' part and know how I felt. And she didn't even take the time to read it. She just threw the book on the floor, and then everybody laughed, and I suddenly hated it. I hated this room full of people who were nearly intelligent, marginally famous, nearly beautiful, who would do nothing but have a good guffaw if they saw me reading Ezra Pound by the pool at the Beverly Wilshire."

"He has read Ezra Pound by every goddamned pool in the world. He does it to prove that he's better than anybody else, people who don't know or care who Ezra Pound was."

"How did it all end?"

"Badly, as you can imagine. We may have had it pointed out to us that it was time to go home. I don't know. It was quite late when we left, and it was all very, very ugly."

"This doesn't sound at all in your line of behavior."

"I have never knowingly insulted anybody in my life. When I say my prayers at night, the list of people who come after '. . . and God bless' is endless. I think of every person I have ever loved every day and I hold them dear in my heart at every moment. Last night I would have hit them with tennis rackets. I would have beaten Carmela with switches all the way down Rexford Drive."

"And today?"

"I am filled with profound regret and remorse."

"I don't do guilt," said Margot. "It'll blow over by cocktail time. Nobody was injured or died?"

"I don't think so. No official body count was taken."

"Then everything's okeydokey. Call Delia and say you're sorry and that's an end to it. I'm leaving you now, so don't panic if your hand feels empty. I'm just sitting here trying to remember what color your eyes are."

"They're pink. Like a rabbit's."

"They're blue," said Carmela. "Blue as sapphires. Well, cheap sapphires."

"Rooney, I have one thing to say to you. It's a long life. Sometimes, parties last longer than a single lifetime. You better be careful. You have the gene in you. My father had it, God rest him. My brothers have it. You have it, too."

"What gene?"

"You know as well as I do." She patted my leg. "Now, off. And she doesn't work in a truck stop. She details cars. She's an auto gloss engineer. Bye for now."

She moved off, her espadrilles squeaking on the pool deck. The gene. In me. I knew exactly what she meant.

I turned to Carmela, who had covered her face with her yellow towel. "I can't tell you how sorry I am."

"Don't tell me. Tell Delia and Buzzy, if they'll answer the phone."

I went in to telephone. I watched Steve McQueen stub out a cigarette before going in to be pounded and kneaded by the Finn. He probably smoked during his massage. He was that cool.

Later on, two years later, I had engraved cards made at Tiffany that said:

Mr. _____ deeply regrets
His behavior of last evening
And begs your indulgence.

But that was later, when the incidents became both more frequent and more outlandish. *Egregious* might be the word I'm after. Incidents of mortification became more and more frequent, fueled by money, by a general malaise, a hatred of almost everything and everybody, even the people I loved the best.

I used to say, "I have to . . ." all the time. Not just, "I have to go to California next week," but, "I have to go to the Callaways for dinner."

Life had become such a burden. Everything irritated me, and nothing so much as myself. *Chacun à son dégoût.*

Buzzy answered on the second ring, as though he had been waiting for my call. He was completely alert. His head didn't throb. His house was spotless, the cleaning people having shown up within two hours after the cocaine was all gone and the guests had left.

He didn't smoke. He didn't drink or do drugs. Said he'd tried them once in college and didn't like them, so he never did them again. Tried them once. I said to him, "You think it was easy for us? We had to work at this, you know." He was a doctor, so he knew things. He had given me my last physical and his only advice when it was all over was, "Change lanes."

"Buzzy. Did anybody die last night?"

"The final count is not in, but it appears the night passed without casualties."

"Any collateral damage?"

"You know that rug in the hall? The one that was made two hundred years ago in Persia?"

"Pretty thing. I like it."

"Liked."

"Gone? Just like that?"

"Well, not exactly just like that. You set fire to it, testing the flammability of Poire Wilhem."

"I set fire to your rug."

"Besides telling Laszlo he was an amateur, you had time for other sports."

"Can it be repaired?"

"I wouldn't know. Maybe the people at the landfill could tell you."

"I feel terrible."

"You're a piece of shit, did anybody ever tell you that?"

"All the time, Buzzy. All the time. You know why? It's the truth. Let me buy you dinner."

"Why don't you buy me a rug?"

"How big?"

"Three feet eight inches by eight feet six inches. Musso's?"

"Eight o'clock."

I spent the afternoon at Aga John's, on Melrose, where I found a Tabriz, silk, an astonishing six hundred knots per square inch. It was the only one they had that was the right size, so I got it and had it delivered. $42,000. Delivery another $300.

Dinner was delightful. The rug was never mentioned, and we all went home and slept like babies.

Carmela and I caught the noon flight from LAX and arrived at midnight, went home, made love in a mad rush before the sleeping pills kicked in, and I bounced out of bed at six, to meet Bart the trainer.

The weekend had cost a total of $50,000, rug included.

I made the money back by lunchtime. I bit the bullet and bought Carmela a diamond and ruby bracelet at Cartier for $78,000 plus tax. A steel plant in Des Moines went bankrupt, but at least my marriage was temporarily intact.

As I said, in those days we were vampires. Charming, glittering vampires.

CHAPTER EIGHT

The Origin of the Species

❖　❖　❖

I had meant to be an artist. It didn't much matter what kind of artist, it was just that there was something inside of me that needed to be expressed, some beautiful and true thing that would explain everything, about me, about the world I was making for myself, about my love for my family and my fellows, and I couldn't find the words or way to get it out, to make it sensible. It was a simple thing. I knew that. Like, "I love you," but that wasn't it. It was deeper than love. It was something primal and true and old, yet still fresh as the first slash of alizarin crimson on a newly gessoed canvas. It was near, always near, but always just out of reach. All I had was the requiem for the thing that needed to be said.

I had a recurring nightmare all through my childhood. In the dream, which came to me almost every night, I had something terribly wrong with me, some incurable and painful ailment, but when I opened my mouth, in the dream, to describe the ailment or to cry for help, no words came out. I was mute to my own pain, unable to explain it or make it go away. I would wake up, covered in sweat, gasping for air, making guttural animal sounds in my throat. Sweat would film my face, and I would sit up in my bed and wait for first light, mute and ill and terrified.

After I graduated from college, I went to Europe for two years, on an extremely prestigious fellowship my parents could never remember the name of. Two years abroad, in England, France, Italy, and Greece. In London, I took figure drawing classes day after day. I took acting classes at night. On Wednesdays, I went to an old Polish crone who pounded the floor with her cane and begged me to play Chopin the way the Master would have wanted. Every Wednesday, I could not, and I could feel her disappointment turning into irritation.

One Wednesday, she whacked my knuckles so hard with her cane that she broke one of my fingers, and, at that moment, I knew that the Master and I would never be friends, so, so long Madame Lutevya, and I moved, splinted, to Florence to be closer to the great painters I aspired to be one of.

It was a joke, spending my mornings at the Uffizi, my afternoons banging away at one canvas after another. Views of the Arno at sunset. Street scenes of Florence. Gypsy children, begging. The kind of paintings you might see for sale on the Ponte Vecchio, but not as good. I had, in my head, images of such beauty and truth and, on my easel, one mess after another. I finally ripped the canvases from the stretchers and threw every one in the coal-burning stove that heated my freezing apartment. I never painted or played the piano again. I couldn't play "Chopsticks" now, if you paid me a million dollars.

My voice stayed mute, the words I meant to say frozen in my throat and in my heart, unknown even to me.

I finally, in a flash, decided that, if I couldn't be eloquent, could never be any more than mediocre, I could at least be rich. So, the return to the States and Wharton and the poker game and my entry into the fray, and, within months, I was unrecognizable, even to myself.

I was vicious, venal, self-absorbed, and totally lacking in feeling. Mea culpa. And I couldn't put my finger on how this had happened, and I couldn't shake the guilt that accompanied it.

I went to church on Sundays, the only one of my friends to do so, and, every Sunday morning, in my high-gloss shoes and my Armani suit, kneeling in my pew on the side of the church, always alone, always far enough from my nearest neighbor that I couldn't be touched or engaged, the tears welled up in my eyes as I sat among the righteous and the chosen, knowing that I was forever shut out from their companionship. I would pray that I would somehow find my way out of this gilded hell I was living in, that I was creating day by day, every day more and more incarcerated in a life I never meant to happen.

But The Street was the ultimate seduction, the beautiful woman who slid into bed with you, naked and perfumed and ravenous. Like the woman, The Street crawled under your skin, and never let you go until it had what it wanted, which was everything you had of a heart and a soul, and no amount of church-going was going to stop that tidal wave of mutual greed. Because I, to my shame, I wanted what The Street offered, the ultimate clusterfuck, the big prize, the endless orgasm.

It's useless to say I didn't know any better. My skin crawled every day, and my nights were haunted by booze and raucous chicaneries, but there was never enough booze or drugs for me to forget that I was being unfaithful to the man I had meant to be, the man I had hoped to become.

Some nights, the elusive thing that so needed to be said was like a fishbone caught in my throat, and I took a Valium and a Scotch until the feeling passed. I would be forever mute.

It's almost never done in the Episcopal Church, but I went to confession. It took place in the priest's office. He put on his stole, we prayed for a while, and then he asked me what my sin was that I had come to confess.

"Despair," I said. "I have put money before kindness or conscience, and it's eating me alive."

"What do you do?"

"I'm a trader downtown. I'm not a good person, not anymore. I have done illegal things. Immoral. That's not even what bothers me. What bothers me is the person it's made me, the person I am. I don't belong in your congregation."

"Despair is the one sin that removes you from God's love."

"I'm afraid all the time."

"Of what?"

"I don't know. Everything. Nothing. My face in the mirror." I could feel the sweat dripping down the back of my neck. I felt sick with vulnerability. Not a feeling I was used to, and not one I liked.

"You must find hope in your heart."

"What heart?"

"You have to look for it." He smiled. "It's there. Trust me."

"I've become everything I despise. Where would I look for hope?"

"God does not abandon you. Ever. You abandon God,

and you must look for him. In the eyes of the poor. In the lost, the less fortunate. Even in the eyes of people who are happy, content with their lot."

He put his hands on my head, a feeling I have loved since childhood, and prayed over me for a long time. He said, reading from the sweet old *Book of Common Prayer*, "'*O Lord*, we beseech thee, mercifully hear our prayers, and spare all those who confess their sins unto thee; that they, whose consciences by sin are accused, by thy merciful pardon may be absolved; through Christ our Lord. *Amen.*

"'*O most* mighty God, and merciful Father, who hast compassion upon all men, and who wouldest not the death of a sinner, but rather that he should turn from his sin, and be saved; Mercifully forgive us our trespasses; receive and comfort us, who are grieved and wearied with the burden of our sins. Thy property is always to have mercy; to thee only it appertaineth to forgive sins. Spare us therefore, good Lord, spare thy people, whom thou hast redeemed; enter not into judgment with thy servants; but so turn thine anger from us, who meekly acknowledge our transgressions, and truly repent us of our faults, and so make haste to help us in this world, that we may ever live with thee in the world to come; through Jesus Christ our Lord. *Amen.*'"

And then this: "'*The Lord* bless us, and keep us. The *Lord* make his face to shine upon us, and be gracious unto us. The *Lord* lift up his countenance upon us, and give us peace, both now and evermore. *Amen.*'"

The priest took his soft hands from my head, and sat back down again.

"Your penance is very simple, and yet you will find it hard. Pay attention. Pay attention to the beauty of God's world around you. Pay attention to the striving life in every eye. Your salvation is not in yourself. It's in other people, and the glory of the world. *Pay. Attention.* You've slumbered too long."

I waited, tears in my eyes. "That's all," he said. "Go now, back into the world, into your life. Never forget this moment."

On the way out, I stuffed all the cash I had into the poor box, hundreds, and, for the whole rest of the day, I felt better, as though I belonged in the human race again.

It didn't last. Does it ever? You pay attention, but the mind wanders.

Salvation is not an easy thing, when the sex is so available, and the lines are chopped out on the table, and you know in your heart that whatever happens, you are lost beyond any penance, any redemption.

My fault, you say? Say what you will. I no longer care. I have done my penance. I have paid attention. Believe me, I have paid.

CHAPTER NINE

The Wages of Sin

❖ ❖ ❖

The truth is, we all hated every single thing we had to do to make the ridiculous amounts of money we made. Stupid money, Fanelli called it. Selling long. Selling short. Betting on the come. Advising people to put all their money into a stock we knew would bounce high like a basketball and then plummet like a sinker on the end of a baited line. As long as The Firm made money on the bounce.

Screaming. The perfect metaphor for what was happening inside our souls. Screaming on the floor all day long, hungry to turn the deal that would cheat a fellow worker and a friend out of a lousy thousand bucks.

We had come, by and large, from modest backgrounds. Houses composed of less square footage than the lofts we now occupied. Our parents would have been ashamed of us if they knew what we did all day long. They would have been mortified if they knew what we paid for some genius to come to our lofts and cut our hair once a week. They would have been terrified to see us wake up at six, lying next to somebody whose name we couldn't quite recall, those we hadn't managed to scoot out the door in the cold light of dawn, used and discarded like opened soup cans. We didn't even walk them down to help them get a cab in the rain.

They were anonymous, already gone from my life, facing the long ride back uptown. Walking into their apartments and slinking by their roommates—also just home from evenings just like theirs—realizing, for the first time perhaps, or the thousandth, that this night just past and the others like it were who they had become. These nights they would try hard to forget, the scrawled numbers they would throw away, knowing that if they called, we wouldn't even remember who they were. And they would sleep for an hour, and then go off to their jobs in publishing houses, at Sotheby's, at *Vogue,* where they spent all day choosing bracelets for their bosses to review.

And we, standing under the scalding shower, realizing that we had gone to all the trouble to seduce these beauties, only to wash their smells off our skin as soon as the door closed behind them, the memory of them vanishing in lather and running down the drain.

The nights when it was just easier to order Chinese and the dealer and a hooker, who at least knew the score, who didn't have to have it explained to them, who at least gave value for the money.

This was us, this was who we were.

Viciousness. Mendacity. Manipulation. Promiscuity. Pour on a little milk, and that is what we ate for breakfast. The trainer at six, who ran his finger across our brow and tasted the sweat, then told us what and how much we had to drink the night before.

And, because we so hated the way we made the money we made, we did our best to get rid of it as fast as we could. If you made $1.5 million a year, you spent $1.7, which, as any Dickensian will tell you, is a formula for misery and degradation.

Forty or forty. Our theme song. Our banner. Our indictment. We didn't care how we got there, we didn't care about collateral damage.

My parents in Virginia would not have recognized me, even though Wharton had been my father's idea in the first place. They lived on in the house where my mother was born, where she had polished the banister for forty years.

I hired a housekeeper for them, and of course the house-keeper did nothing right, didn't do anything the way my mother liked, and she was gone after six weeks.

They kept my bedroom for me, thinking I would come to stay with them for Christmas, a room that was filled with my track and field trophies, my letter jacket hanging in the closet, a picture of me and a girl named Ashleigh Conaway, head of the cheerleading squad, on the desk, she in a strapless gown, her hair done up in a French twist, a corsage of crimson and white carnations on her wrist, our school colors, off to the prom, which meant nothing to me except that I might get the chance, if I got her drunk enough, to fuck her in my father's car. In the picture, I am wearing a tuxedo in which there are condoms in the pocket, but you can't see that, you see only two young people, arms around each other's waists, off to a prom maybe or maybe not to get lucky.

My mother forwarded to me a letter she got addressed to me, and it was from a girl in my class who wrote movingly of a clear memory she had of a homecoming dance she went to alone, because she was obese, and thanking me because I was the only boy there who asked her to dance, shaming me with the heated realization that there was once in me a kindness that I had effectively killed on the trading floor. She told me she had lost a hundred pounds. That she was happy now, married with three, and with a view of the Rockies out her kitchen window. I never answered. The person to whom the letter was written no longer existed.

I told my parents there was a room for them in my loft, knowing that they would never come. New York frightened them. When it came down to it, *I* frightened them, even more than the filthy, teeming city.

They didn't understand a life in which home was simply the place to which you went to change your shirt and phone for the limo. In the entire five thousand square feet, there was not one comfortable chair. It wasn't to be lived in, it was to be photographed, to open its doors only to lonely girls or crowds of a hundred, who came to watch the Super Bowl.

And I can't express how thrilling it all was. Watching white-coated waiters, any one of whom could have been in a contest to choose the most beautiful waiter in the world, serving mojitos to men and women, any one of whom might have graced the cover of *Vogue* or *Men's Health*. My mother imagined me with a girl who would have been on the cover of *Good Housekeeping,* and here I was with women whose IQ often was equal to twice their weight, brilliant, slender girls on their way up, girls who were like racehorses in their beauty, if not their lineage. So sleekly groomed. Such silky hair.

Here I was, knowing that deep in the bowels of my

building was parked a Lamborghini of which there were only twelve in the world. Knowing that in London there were shoemakers and tailors who had my measurements on file, my tables at Christmas littered with cards, most of them from shopkeepers.

It couldn't last. We were bright enough to know that. We accepted that. The pace was too fast. The fire was too hot not to burn out. But, God, who, in our position, wouldn't walk around with an erection twenty-four hours a day? We were in our late twenties and early thirties.

Forty or forty. It was our curse. It was our blessing. It was our mantra. We were simply the people we were described as being. Big Swinging Dicks. And we hated ourselves and we loved ourselves and the world would survive our shenanigans no matter how much destruction we sowed.

And the thing, the thing I had meant to say, got forgotten, leaving me mute as a stone in the gilded desert.

CHAPTER TEN

Fanelli Does Funtown

❖ ❖ ❖

S o, Fanelli wanted to go to Vegas for the night in the worst kind of way. I stopped by his office for a smoke and heard him on the phone with the travel agent. He was yelling.

"Listen, hon," he bellowed. "Doll. Maybe I didn't make myself clear. I want to rent, I want waiting at the curb at the airport, a white convertible El Dorado. Did you get that? White. I want the biggest, baddest Cadillac fucking El Dorado there is to be had, and it better be there the second the plane lands and it better be fucking white." He slammed down the phone. "I *love* dealing with the simple American public!"

"Fanelli," I said. "I can understand wanting a Cadillac. I can understand the convertible part. But why white?"

He looked at me with that gesture of his hands, wide away from his body, that indicated my-God-you-can-be-so-stupid-it-appalls-me, and he said in his most condescending tone. "Black for Tahoe. White for Vegas."

The reason Fanelli wanted to go to Vegas was that Fanelli was arranging his own bachelor party. Fanelli was getting married, and as he said, he didn't trust the rest of us mindless jerks to arrange it. "I mean, Cubans and steaks in the cigar room at Frank's and then on to Billy's Topless. What kind of shit is *that*?"

Fanelli was getting married because he had fallen in love during the Hamptons summer with an English girl named Anthea. Anthea worked in an advertising agency, which seemed incredibly glamorous to us, although she said she did it mainly because she could wear painter's pants and ripped men's T-shirts to work and nobody said a thing. Obsessed as we were with the finer points of Italian tailoring, this seemed like a good deal to us, although, when he met her, she was standing at the bar in a gold lamé microskirt and a sheer golden blouse through which you could see the dark aureole of her nipples, and she looked like a model, which is what she used to be before she went back to school and became an art director. "Standing around all day in other people's clothes," was all she had to say about the modeling profession in general.

I think she played the English girl thing a little too hard, and she looked like she had chopped off her hair with a pair of dull paper scissors, but she was a good thing and she could smoke cigars with us and drink almost anybody under the table.

She never went to work before eleven because she had such a strenuous nightlife, and she said that, when her bosses remarked that she was late, she always simply said, "Yes, I am, actually." She said making up excuses was the way to hell because she had to make up so many of them and she had to remember what she'd said the time before and there were only so many times you could say you had to take the dog you didn't have to the vet, or wait for the plumber, and that, anyway, part of her job was to suck up the culture as it was happening at that very moment and then spew it back out in the pages of magazines and flickering TV screens in the half-dark living rooms of Cleveland and Mobile and it wasn't her fault if so much of the culture happened to take place at two in the morning.

Anthea made it through the radar because she was like all the girls who made it through the radar. She was tall. She was thin. She wasn't a total moron. And she brought something to the party, what with her cigar-smoking, Remy-swilling ways. Referring to her weight and her remarkable bone structure she said, "I am a girl composed entirely of dairy products."

So Fanelli had spent $50K on a ring and taken her to Chantarelle and they were going to be married in two weeks. I was going to be a groomsman.

They were in fact, going to be married twice, once in New York and once, the following summer, in England, where of course her parents were some sort of landed gentry and lived in some enormous, drafty pile and everybody would show up in hats and morning jackets and drink sherry on the lawn before the wedding, which would be performed by dear Vicar somebody or other.

She knew everybody in the fashion world. Geoffrey Beene was making her wedding dress. Kevyn Aucoin was doing her makeup. He's dead now. Painkiller overdose, after making so many cadaverous girls look so fabulous.

So steaks and topless bars seemed a little underwhelming to Fanelli. He was in love, and vowed that once he was married he was going to change his ways and become a regular person and move to Greenwich and have children who would have two middle names in that English way and he just wouldn't be available on the let's-go-to-William's-on-Carmine-Street-and-pick-up-an-eight-ball circuit anymore. So he wanted Vegas for one night.

He wanted Vegas and everything it had to offer in the way of illicit, drunken, lewd behavior.

Anthea, who hauled in $200K a year just to make girls' hair shine, not bad cash for a twenty-six-year-old visitor to our shores, was going to Jamaica with three friends for the weekend to dance with Rasta boys and smoke big spliffs and come home completely unnerved by the whole experience. She was really just like one of the guys and that's why we liked her and didn't feel so badly that Fanelli was moving away from us.

So it was Trotmeier, and Frank, who was so large and not small-boned—so big in fact that he had a special clause written into his contract that said he could take a limo to work every morning because he couldn't fit into an ordinary cab, and had to fly first class whenever he traveled on business—and, of course, there was Fanelli and me.

We landed in Las Vegas at three on Saturday afternoon. I was a little peaked, since I'd been up all night the night before with Carmela, having the usual you-don't-love-me-enough discussion, but a couple of gin and tonics and a power nap on the plane had put a little color back in my cheeks. I just didn't feel ready to be festive enough, so I knew I'd have to dig deep and suck it up to get through all the carnage.

Sure enough, there was a big white El Dorado parked at the curb, with a cowering little girl from Hertz holding the keys for Fanelli. He gave her fifty dollars. "See?" said Fanelli. "We're having fun already!"

We pulled up at Caesar's Palace in a big hoopla of vulgarity and testosterone. They'd seen it all before. They didn't raise an eyebrow. Fanelli said Vegas was the only town in the world where you could land, rent a car, stay the weekend, and return the car with less than five miles on it.

We could have taken a cab for a lot less, but Big Frank wouldn't fit, and he would have whinged all the way. That was an English thing Anthea had taught us. "Oh, stop whingeing," she would say, when Frank made a ruckus because his steak wasn't really black and blue.

At the desk they gave me a key to my room, and I asked how to get there. "First you go through the casino," said the key keeper. In Vegas, at Caesar's Palace, to get anywhere you have to go through the casino. "And then you turn right at Cleopatra's Barge, our floating restaurant, and then you walk down the hall until you come to the eighteen-foot statue of Joe Louis and then you turn left and take the elevator up to Room 1812 in the Fantasy Tower." And he was absolutely right.

When we checked in, Fanelli gave us each an envelope and said, "Welcome to Vegas boys. See you for dinner at eight. Look sharp."

This is what Room 1812 looked like: it was really big. It was aqua. It was on two levels.

On the upper level, there was an eight-foot round bed, covered in a burgundy velvet bedspread. There was one chair. On the night table, there was a clock radio that was literally broken in half, as though the previous tenant had taken a pickax to it after a bad night.

There was a single small window, through which you could look out across the desert, except that the window was covered with a cement trellis, so you could just get these tiny little glimpses through the interstices. The window didn't open. They *really* didn't want anybody to get a notion to jump out the window of Room 1812 after a bad night at the tables. No matter how desperate you were, you were not about to jump out of Room 1812 in the Fantasy Tower.

But here's the incredible part. Next to the bed, literally six feet away, on the lower level, there was an eight-foot octagonal, three-foot-deep Jacuzzi, like an above-ground pool. Eighteen stories above ground. I guessed that was the fantasy part of the Fantasy Tower.

I had to search to find the toilet, a tiny closet hidden away on the other side of the room. Everything in there was petite—a tiny toilet, a minuscule shower and sink.

I opened Fanelli's envelope. Inside, there were six condoms, a gram of cocaine, and ten one-hundred-dollar bills, along with a note that said, "Thanks for sharing my last night on earth as we know it." Fanelli was a generous guy.

I tried to lie down for a while and it was then I noticed that directly over the bed there was an equally large mirror. I wouldn't have believed it either, except I was there.

Sleep wouldn't come. I kept thinking of myself floating on the mirrored ceiling, I kept trying to take in the whole of it, the gestalt, and it was just too mind-boggling. I guess Vegas just isn't a nap kind of town.

So I got up, did a few lines of Fanelli's excellent coke, and that perked me right up. I decided to go prowl.

In the casino, there was every kind of craven face you could imagine. There were a lot of fat people. There were a lot of Asians. It smelled like sweat—and money, of which there were vast amounts exchanging hands.

At the slots, there was a seventy-year-old woman at a slot machine in a thin housedress and bedroom slippers relentlessly pulling the handle with a bucket of quarters in front of her and a cigarette dangling from her withered lips.

I thought, how could a habit that is so sexy and attractive in young people be so dirty and repellent in the old? Note to self: Give up smoking at forty. You can behave badly and still be charming and people get over it. Behave unattractively and just watch the velvet ropes go up all over town. I would be the only person in history to give up smoking not for health but for fashion. But I thought: What the hell, I didn't come to Vegas to give up smoking.

I didn't bet in the afternoon. I just wandered around, scoping out the joint. It was vast, and there were no clocks, like in the office, and people were basically behaving like they did on the trading floor. I felt perfectly at home.

I drank cocktails and watched the action. The cool silence of the blackjack table. The heated frenzy of a hot craps table, the sweaty drear of a cold one. The timid bettors, the ones who couldn't not play even knowing they couldn't afford to lose. The expansive ranchers with stacks of black chips sitting in front of them. The honeymoon couples, playing with Daddy's money.

My life seemed so large to me, wandering through the casino; young, with a lot of future and a lot of money and a lot of girls and a gram of cocaine upstairs in the Fantasy Tower. I could feel the pulse of the room. I knew I was going to win and I had time.

There were hookers everywhere. Beautiful girls. But I didn't feel like sex at the moment. I just wanted to be an ordinary American who had flown to Vegas with his best friends and arrived in a white El Dorado with three other rich, good-looking young men to take in the sights. I got sentimental for Fanelli, for his generosity, for his expansive good nature, for the night after night we had sat together drinking and talking about things, not the first one of which I could recall. And laughing. Always laughing at the little people.

I didn't play because I didn't want to lose. I only wanted to win and that would come later. I could feel it in my blood.

I looked at my watch. It was seven o'clock. There was no other way to gauge time. You couldn't look outdoors. At Caesar's Palace, there was no outdoors, and no time.

On my way to my room, I saw a couple in tennis whites come in through one of the smoked glass doors. I looked at them, astonished that there were tennis courts at the hotel, that anybody would come to Vegas to play tennis. The brief glimpse of sky through the sliding doors showed bloodred and pale blue.

Freshly showered and shaved, coked up and wearing a sober blue suit, I showed up for dinner exactly at eight. Dinner was in the Frank Sinatra Room. Everybody else was there, a bottle of $250 Bordeaux uncorked on the table.

It was a little spooky. There were big photographs of Frank and the boys all over the room. All of them are dead now, and even then they were pretty old. They were from another time, a time when Vegas was brand new, when nobody took a pickax to the bedside clock.

"Welcome to the New Rat Pack," said Fanelli as I sat down.

"Frank Sinatra had all his suits made by the same tailor, and they were all lined in orange silk," I said.

"How do you know such an enormous number of useless things?" asked Fanelli.

"Frank Sinatra's tailor made me a suit, when I was in Los Angeles. Ugliest suit I ever had. Lined in orange silk."

Fanelli had had a good day. He'd checked in with a $100 chip in his pocket, left over from an earlier venture in Vegas. Without thinking, on his way to his room, he put the chip on thirty-two, his lucky number, at the first roulette table he passed.

Thirty-two had come in, so he was up thirty-five hundred. He then pulled back, played the corners and the splits, and thirty-six had come in. He pulled back again, left two hundred on thirty-two, and, incredibly enough, thirty-two hit again. He walked away with almost twenty thousand before he put the key in his door. He was feeling expansive, and sentimental.

So he spent three thousand dollars on three hookers, each one a different ethnic persuasion, none of them Caucasian. "I'll have enough of white meat," he said. "Very soon."

Arcane positions. Frothy sex in the overflowing Jacuzzi. He made it all sound hysterically fun, and he did look remarkably refreshed.

The girls had stayed silent long enough for him to call Anthea to tell her how much he adored her. Fanelli felt it was the least he could do, and besides, he did, he really did adore her.

Dinner, which was surprisingly good, was a fountain of expensive libation and unbridled hilarity. Everything seemed right. The company of my best friends, the pictures of Sinatra, the overpriced, overdressed food, the bored waiters who'd seen every kind of behavior man is capable of producing, no doubt, and carried on with a kind of faux hauteur that, in itself, added to the hilarity of it all.

Talk of vintages and women and all the times we'd gotten wrecked together and done strange and funny things, and endless talk of money and how much of it there was to be had in the world. Just put a chip on your lucky number. Let the wheel roll. Like taking candy from a baby.

We gave Fanelli his wedding present. We'd gotten a sterling cigar box at Tiffany's, and had all our signatures engraved on it, and then filled it with Cuban cigars. It brought Fanelli to tears of deep and empathic sentimentality. There was a danger of losing the festivity of the moment, he was so moved, even though he knew Anthea would never let him smoke once they got married. She loathed it.

Frank kept the ball rolling. Frank had awakened one morning not long before, still drunk, and he had had a big meeting early and he was rushing around getting dressed, when he suddenly realized he couldn't remember how to tie a necktie. He kept trying in front of the bathroom mirror. Nothing.

Luckily, Frank was the kind of guy who kept everything he'd ever owned, and he remembered that he had the card that came with his very first necktie, a card that had simple diagrams showing a thirteen-year-old boy how to tie a necktie, and he'd managed to find it, but he still couldn't follow the diagram.

So he'd just draped his best tie around his neck, gone downstairs to hail a cab, and was seated in the back reading the *Journal* when he caught his reflection in the rearview mirror. "My God," he thought, thinking of other things, "I forgot to tie my necktie." And he effortlessly reached up and tied a perfectly dimpled double Windsor without even looking. That's the kind of guy Frank was. Never daunted in public. He walked into the meeting clean shaven, perfectly dressed, a true white-collar drunk, and he performed brilliantly, recommending all kinds of intricate maneuvers to a ski-binding manufacturer who was filthy rich and who started the meeting by looking at Frank and saying, "Young man. Do I look to you like the kind of man who pays taxes?"

There were toasts, in which we wished Fanelli happy days and fair, despite his many, many former indiscretions, most of which were elaborately detailed.

Fanelli stood up and simply said that, after this weekend, as soon as the plane touched down in New York, the Fanelli as we knew him was dead forever, and he would see us at the office and treat us all as the sources of some of the happiest times of his life, but that the life that had been so happy was now a thing of the past. He actually got misty-eyed. He actually said, "I love you guys," which everybody had been hoping he'd avoid, but nevertheless, we were all moved nearly to tears, and we embraced Fanelli and then he paid for dinner in cash, leaving a tip that caused the waiters to view Fanelli in a whole new light, and then we went to see Diana Ross in the Colosseum, the Big Room.

It was kind of a homosexual thing to do, and we sat in our red velvet banquette realizing that we looked like a bunch of gay guys from the Midwest come to worship at the feet of the Diva. Many, many cocktails were served and consumed in absolute silence as we stared at this creature, this remarkable thing that was called Diana Ross. And I'm telling you, that woman could *sing,* I don't care how mean she was to the other girls or how she let them go on welfare while she stood in front of an adoring audience in a red se-quined dress and a coat made out of white feathers.

"I bet she gives great head," said Frank, and Trotmeier answered, "She must never eat anything, to stay so skinny."

Fanelli said, "I feel like I'm turning a little bit gay, just watching her." He had a weird fetish, Fanelli. He carried with him, everywhere he went, a four-inch stuffed bear, a model of one of the characters on *Sesame Street,* Fozzie

Bear. Fozzie had been to Europe, Grand Cayman, around the globe, and Fanelli had photographed him in all these exotic locations, and kept an album of Fozzie's travels. Fozzie at the Eiffel Tower. Fozzie at the Kremlin. He had photographed every one of his friends with Fozzie, and gave Fozzie a birthday party every year, with a Fozzie cake and everything. He gave a Fozzie to every woman he slept with, after taking a photograph of the girl and the bear.

Bears make money, said Fanelli. Bears also get laid.

Now Fozzie sat with a bottle of Cristal ringside at Caesar's palace, the bright light from the stage illuminating his green hat, as he watched one of the greatest entertainers ever.

After the show, Fanelli was determined to get a picture of Fozzie and the Diva herself. He somehow wangled his way backstage and, confronted by her enormous security team, told them he was Arne Næss, her Swedish billionaire boyfriend whom she married the next year, and he actually made his way into Diana's dressing room, and took the picture. She thought the whole thing was charming and couldn't have been nicer about it. She laughed with delight, showing her millions of gleaming teeth. It was the victory of his and Fozzie's career.

After the Diana adventure, we went our separate ways,

our pockets filled with cash, each one just waiting for the adrenaline to kick in and take over everything, every desire, every dream, every tic of our overwrought nervous systems. Just for the spin of a wheel. Just for the slap of a card on the green felt table. Just for the roll of the dice. Just like Monday morning at the office. Except it was one o'clock in the morning in Vegas. But it was exactly the same.

I lost a thousand playing blackjack, too taken with the dealer, who was really hot in her dealer's getup, to pay much attention to the cards.

I put a hundred on thirty-two at roulette, just for Fanelli, and lost.

Then I saw this kind of woebegone craps table that looked like it needed a little love. There were only about six people at the table, all clearly losers. I thought, OK, guys, step aside and let the big dog eat.

I stepped up to the table and took a place next to the croupier. I cashed in five hundred. I lost four hundred in two minutes. Then the dice came to me, and everything clicked on. Cowboy up, I thought.

I threw the dice. Six. I started throwing and betting and pushing and I could do no wrong. Every throw was exactly the number I needed. I could envision the numbers before the dice landed.

I was playing the odds. Six came up. I threw for a new number. Seven. I threw again. Five. I kept throwing and the crowd at the table began to grow. The pile of chips in front of me was growing, so I began betting more recklessly.

I turned to tip the croupier. "Just put fifty on the come line for me, kid. That'll be enough."

I did it, and from then on, the croupier and I were in it together. I would bet for me, and he would tell me what to do with his chips. This never happens in Vegas, where the croupiers are supposed to be absolutely silent. He started giving me advice on how to improve my odds.

Cocktails began to appear on the table in front of me. I must have told one of the toga-clad girls what I was drinking, but I have no recollection of it. They just started appearing. And more people came, and there was a buzz, a heat that began to swell into an inferno.

There were guys who followed my every move, with stacks of black chips, betting five hundred dollars on me, and I was in tune, in perfect sync with the rhythm of the table. I was always one step ahead of fate.

After twenty minutes, there were probably fifty people at the table. Fanelli stopped by. I didn't even see him. Frank stepped up and played along. I didn't know he was there, even though he was gigantic. There was nothing in the world except me and the dice and the long stretch of green baize, sprinkled with numbers and spaces and littered with money.

They changed croupiers, trying to throw me off. They brought more cocktails. A tall, lanky whore in a sparkly dress came and stood next to me, her thigh touching mine as I leaned forward to toss the dice. I just wasn't interested.

I rolled for forty-five minutes. I went through three croupiers, until the original croupier came back. I was betting for two again, and nothing went wrong for a long, long time.

When I crapped out, after forty-five minutes, the table applauded. There were nine gin and tonics lined up in front of me.

The croupier turned to me. "Here's what you do now, kid. Let two people roll. If you don't win, pick up your chips and walk away from the table. You've had a good night. Walk away from it."

Pigs lose everything.

The next roller was a small Asian man. He looked like loss in a size-36 suit. I lost five hundred. The dice moved into the hands of a man who looked like John Carradine in one of his wilder roles—a Mormon preacher gone berserk. He threw once. I lost.

"That's it for you, kid," the croupier said, and I gathered up my chips, turned to tip him a hundred.

"Trust me, kid. You've done enough for me. Just say good night." When I left the table, you could see the high rollers gathering up their chips, moving on, knowing that things like this don't happen very often, hardly ever, and that this table was in for a long, cold spell.

I turned to the dark-haired hooker standing next to me. "Room 1812. Fantasy Tower. Ten minutes."

I picked up my chips, and stuffed them in every pocket. The Italians say never put anything in the pocket of your suit, it'll blow the line. I made an exception.

I took three gin and tonics, and went to cash out. I had made $32,000.

In fifteen minutes I was naked on the maroon bed with the hooker who turned out to be named Arrielle. She spelled it for me. *Yeah,* I thought. *And I'm Billy Champagne. I've got $32,000 in cash and I can be anybody I want.*

I don't love having sex with hookers. They don't like to kiss, for one thing. Their breasts are beyond fake. There's something listless about it, knowing that one of you is bored out of her mind, staring at her reflection in the mirror over our heads and going over her list of errands for the next day. But I gave her oral sex, which I was a whiz at, never a false step, and she seemed to like that. She scratched at my back with her long, black nails.

You can make love to a hooker in less time than it takes to listen to a Top 40 song. When it was done, I gave her two thousand dollars, and she absolutely loved that part. Now she could go home for the rest of the night.

At the door, she turned to me, still lying naked on the bed. She wagged her finger at me and winked, "Some lucky girl . . ." was all she said, and then she was gone.

I took a bath. It took twenty minutes to fill the goddamned thing, but I did it, dragging on cigarettes and drinking gin and tonic.

The water calmed me down. It soothed my heart. You could have done laps in the pool. It was the perfect end to a lovely night.

I lay down on the covers, smoking a last cigarette and finishing the cocktails. I caught sight of myself in the mirror above me, lying damp and naked on the velvet. I was suddenly in love with myself.

There was no trace left of the boy I had been. I was a fully formed man with a perfect body. I could see the thick veins on my biceps, my washboard stomach, my thighs, my crotch, my wet hair cut at an ungodly cost every three weeks by a small British man named Benjamin Moss who came to my loft, and I adored myself, and I was as fine at that moment as I would ever be. My parents, far away, would be shocked and appalled. My mother, if she knew the course of this evening's events, would come and get me and take me home and make me behave.

The sun was just coming up and the room turned all

rosy and romantic, garish as it was. I fell asleep without even getting under the covers, with the last wisp of cigarette smoke hanging in the air and thirty thousand dollars of house money on the bedside table, right next to the pickaxed alarm clock. I love this town, I thought.

I knew that no dawn would ever rise again so beautifully, no matter what happened.

Three hours later, the phone rang. It was Fanelli. "In two minutes, room service will be at your door with Bloody Marys, and I'll be right with them. Get dressed."

A few minutes later I was at the door in my Paul Stuart boxers and there was Fanelli and, immediately after, a white-coated room service cutie with three Bloody Marys.

"Wakey wakey eggs and bakey," shouted Fanelli. "Isn't this fun? Isn't this just the most fun you've ever had?"

He gave the girl twenty dollars for her trouble, and she left us alone to drink and tell the tales while I dressed. Fozzie had his own Bloody Mary, and Fanelli dutifully photographed it.

Fanelli sat on the edge of the Jacuzzi. "This is the biggest ashtray I have ever seen in my life," he said, flicking a cigar ash into it.

"What time is it?" I asked.

"Who the hell cares? It's time to go lie by the pool and get a little color in our pallid cheeks so Anthea won't think

I spent all my time getting blowjobs from black hookers, which actually is what I mostly did, except that I had time to win fifty thou and change at roulette. How'd you do?"

"One white girl named Arrielle, working at being a hooker so she can pay for childcare for the twins. Thirty thousand. Craps."

"Not bad," he shouted. "Not bad at all. Now let's go have a big breakfast and then some sun. And then off to the airport. No more gambling. Know when to walk away, that's the whole secret. Try it again, they get it all back and we don't want that to happen now, do we?"

"We do not, Fanelli," I said. "We do not want that to happen."

We met Trotmeier and Frank, and sat at breakfast, placing the occasional bet with the strolling Keno girls, and we told the night again and again. Everybody had won money. Fanelli, of course, had won the most. I came in second, then Frank, then Trotmeier who had only won a puny six thousand dollars because he lacked the lightning rod that attracted the bolt from the blue, he always had, which is why he made the least of us at the office, although, by normal standards, he made plenty for somebody who was only twenty-nine years old. But cautious.

I thought of Arrielle, sleeping at home. I thought of Diana Ross, in a grand suite on a high floor. It always amazes me that people have sex, even desultory sex, and then go on with their lives, eating scrambled eggs, telling jokes, as though nothing had happened. It seems such a ravishing experience. Such a miracle. And I kept thinking of the sight of my own body in the circular mirror, a kind of sex all its own. And yet there I was, here were my friends, and last night was already past and gone forever, like a wisp of smoke in the dawn light.

We lay by the pool, in our surfer shorts and our Oakleys. We dozed and drank cocktails and said very little. Then it was noon and time to pack and go.

I threw my few things in a bag and took one last look at Room 1812, to remember every detail. I hadn't even pulled back the covers on the bed.

Fanelli threw a hundred on number thirty-two as we passed a table. He lost. "You see?" he said. "It heats up. It cools down. Let's hit the road."

In the first-class cabin, we settled into our leather seats. The stewardess asked what we wanted to drink. "I don't know," said Frank. "Our bodies are wrecked but our minds want to boogie. What do you have for that?"

She brought each of us three Remys.

At the last minute, an airline attendant appeared at Fanelli's seat. "Are you Mr. Fanelli?" she asked.

"Yes."

"You left this at the ticket counter," she said, and handed him his battered briefcase.

"Thank you," said Fanelli, calm as a cuke, and then opened the briefcase. The fifty thousand was still there in cash. "Thank you very much," peeling off a hundred and giving it to her.

"You see," he said. "I love this town."

The plane took off and headed east. This day, this particular perfection, would last forever. Nothing could touch it, the warmth and humor of my friends, the easy roll of the dice, the stack of cash, the beginning of my life as a man.

It wasn't true, of course. It didn't last forever, or very long at all, really. Nothing does. I never saw Vegas again. I never rode in a white El Dorado with the top down. Two months later I was fired. Trotmeier burned out and became the tame manager of a branch bank somewhere. Frank was sitting at his desk on a beautiful September morning two months shy of his fortieth birthday and retirement, just waiting for his settlement package to kick in, just sitting in his office on the eighty-ninth floor, when the first plane hit.

Only Fanelli went on, married to Anthea, fathering one beautiful child after another, hitting on thirty-two in London and Cannes and Monaco.

But at that moment, warmed by cash and Remy in the sun-blasted first-class cabin, I felt invincible. I loved the feeling of the movement of my body inside my clothes. I felt like the Christ child floating in the warm amniotic waters of his mother's womb.

Yes, that's it. I felt like the little baby Jesus, just waiting to be born on Christmas Day.

CHAPTER ELEVEN

Ball Gowns of the Eighties

❖ ❖ ❖

You want to know the difference between a mouse and a rat? Here it is, simple. If the rodent is in your apartment, no matter how large and voracious it may be, it's a mouse. If it's in *my* apartment, no matter how small and timid, it's a rat. Now let me tell you about Alexis Tayloe. In the first place, she was in my apartment.

To be specific, she was standing in my apartment wearing a navy blue satin ball gown made by Oscar de la Renta, with the $12,000 price tag still hanging from a beaded sleeve. Satin, as women are always telling you, is the cruelest fabric to wear, and Alexis Tayloe did not look particularly good in this creation, but there she was. In my apartment.

And she had breast cancer.

These two facts were in no way related, and only one fact, the price of the dress, was certifiably true. Perhaps I should go back a bit.

I went to one of those almost-but-not-quite Ivy League schools. The first night I was there, I noticed that almost all of my hallmates were wearing sweatshirts from the schools they really wanted to go to—Harvard, Cornell, Princeton, schools they had worked their whole lives to get into and then been turned away from with a banging of the door that was the first irrevocable failure of their young lives. The air was filled with the silent memory of opening that letter that said, basically, we were eighteen and already losers for life.

In my last year at what I quickly learned to call "university" instead of the more prosaic "college," when I won the fellowship, my girlfriend, who was two inches taller than I was and as beautiful as a sunrise, won the same fellowship, and we set off to have adventures, sailing to England on the *France,* in one of its last crossings, and we spent the year in London, she in drama school, I in art, a practice for which I had tremendous zeal and almost no talent. We did nothing but fight and have our hair cut at Sweeney's on Beauchamp Place. We lived in a rented room, the former tenant of which had been Heathcote Williams, the nervous-breakdown-riddled playwright, and we slept in a single bed from which you could see where Heathcote had written "Good Old Shortass" on the ceiling. One wondered during which nervous breakdown it had occured to him to stand on a chair with a Magic Marker in order to write that.

When we were happy, we stopped people dead on the street with our youth and loveliness. When we were unhappy, we lay in our single bed, trying not to touch each other's skin, the light from outside the window illuminating Heathcote's strange greeting.

Somewhere along the way, I met Alexis Tayloe. She was older than I was by maybe ten years, and she had a dull husband named Cyril who was always standing for a seat in Parliament somewhere. They were very rich, and had an immaculate townhouse on Onslow Square. Alexis was a graduate student of something obscure, and spent all her days in the British Library. They had a baby, who was attended almost solely by a live-in nanny. Alexis would study all day, and then have dinner out with friends, and then go home, where she would rush up to the nursery and wake the baby to embrace her and sing her a lullaby, even though she was already happily sound asleep. The baby, Olympia, developed a severe rash that wouldn't go away, and the doctors determined that the rash was caused by being awakened in the middle of the night by a virtual stranger to be showered with kisses and off-key singing. She literally did not know who her own mother was. The result was that Alexis was told to leave the baby alone altogether.

So, Alexis and I met in a restaurant, while my girlfriend was rehearsing late for a production of some esoteric Jacobean play. The rehearsals often ran very late and, when she came home, I could tell she had been kissing somebody because her look was sly and her lips were puffy, and because, when she got into bed, she would immediately hug the wall and turn her head away. Some things you don't need a diagram to understand. You just know.

So Alexis and I met, and after one of these dinners while the girlfriend was off making puffylips with some Bohemian theater person, Alexis and I got into a cab and rode around Hyde park for four hours, making love, something that gave me a special thrill, such a frisson of erotic play that I remember every kiss to this day. Fucking in a London cab is like making love in a sensory deprivation tank, except that the tank is moving and the meter is running. Alexis always paid, of course. Sometimes the fare was ten pounds, if she felt guilty about the baby, and sometimes it was sixty. Fucking in a London taxicab is not a memory that leaves you, ever, and we got into the habit of doing it two or three times a week, after which I would go home and crawl into bed with what might as well have been a six-foot two-by-four with puffy lips.

We never spoke of it. We just fought more, and every time we had a fight, we would get our hair cut at Sweeney's, until eventually we were not only beautiful but perhaps the two most finely coiffed people in London.

I ran out of money, and the girlfriend moved in with the director of the Jacobean lip puffer, and my father refused to send me a penny, instead sending me a letter advising that I give up my pretensions to art and come home and do something solid, like go to business school. I could always paint as a hobby, he said, act in amateur theatricals.

Actually, Sweeney's on Beauchamp Place was where the most mortifying thing that ever happened to me happened, one of those things that you know, even at the time, will shape your self-image forever. When my very first haircut was over, I tipped the barber an enormous amount, wanting him to think I was some mysterious big shot worthy of his ministrations, and he gave me a brush of a sort I had never seen before and I proceeded to brush my perfect hair with it, until he leaned and whispered in my ear that what he had given me was a clothing brush, sir, with the utmost degree of condescension that an Englishman can muster, which is a vast amount. I determined, from that moment, that I would never be less than accurate in my public behavior, lest I be revealed to be the country hick I, in reality, was. To this day I recall the mortification.

I had run completely out of money, so Alexis wrote me a

check for a thousand dollars to get me home. She wrote me the check from her secret dollars account, money that rolled in every month from an accounting firm in Shaker Heights, and I went home, and then on to Wharton, and then to the poker game and then to my first year at The Firm. I never paid Alexis back her thousand dollars. It slipped my mind.

In your first year at The Firm, they paid you hardly anything, on the theory that you didn't have any time to spend money anyway. The day went from six in the morning until after ten at night. At six, they brought in dinner. After ten, there was a fleet of black cars to take you home to your horrible little apartment.

My horrible little apartment was a fifth-floor walkup. With skylights. The ground floor was a Spanish restaurant and the second floor was a Chinese whorehouse, the remaining floors being filled with identical rat-infested apartments. Outside, the streets were alive all through the night with crackheads and hookers. God, New York was so filthy then. It was great. There were drugs everywhere for you to spend your discretionary income—of which there wasn't any—on, and dance clubs that sprang up for two nights and then vanished, only to pop up a week later two doors down the street.

In these clubs, men danced bare-chested together, and the bathrooms were unisex, dark caverns of sin where you could buy pure cocaine while fucking Puerto Rican girls or boys, for whom, I discovered, I had a long-suppressed taste, depending on how I felt that night, or who touched your ass first. This idea of seeing men as objects of sexual desire both excited and terrified me. I kept telling myself I was just experimenting, having fun. I certainly wasn't a homosexual.

But anything was possible. Anything was allowed, suddenly. It was a vibrant cauldron of desire, New York in those days, desire and freedom and garbage—there was garbage everywhere all the time. It has now been totally and completely erased, until all that's left is a mall for luxury goods. I could never understand why anybody would want frozen yogurt when you could have a blowjob in a dark doorway, the same doorway where the crackhead had held the knife to your throat two nights earlier, ripping the gold cross from your neck, leaving marks, and asking as he galloped off to the next rock of crack, "Hey! Is this real gold?" And what would *you* say in that situation?

Anyway, that apartment was known to all my friends as Hovel Hall, and we were all learning to cook out of Julia Child then, so I would prepare and serve boeuf braise Prince Albert while rats slunk beneath the stove. I made croquembouche in that apartment at three a.m., high on coke and gin, a recipe that started out, "First, make 306 cream puffs."

And here was Alexis Tayloe, that first summer, in a blue satin ball gown and a tumor in her breast. Or so she said.

You have to understand that nobody ever spent the

night at Hovel Hall. Ever. A friend had given me guest towels on which he had had embroidered, "Don't be here when I wake up," and now Alexis Tayloe's bras were hanging over the rack of my shower stall. I had forgotten to pay her back her fucking thousand Shaker Heights dollars, so what choice, when she wrote from London and said she wanted to stay with me, did I have? Zilch choice, that's what.

She had appeared with two enormous suitcases, and told me immediately that she had long since ceased to love me (I never knew she did in the first place), and that she had breast cancer and had come to New York, filthy, gorgeous New York, *my* New York, my sexy, drugged out, work-like-a-dog and play-like-a-tiger New York, for radiation treatments at Mt. Sinai. And so began our short life together.

I would get up at five every day, be at the office by six, scream and yell and feint and parry all day long with my fellow conspirators, until we had no voices left, then go out and eat chicken wings at some bar and get drunk on well vodka, and then I would go home after midnight, sometimes puking in the cab, often losing the coke on the floor of some darkened unisex bathroom downtown.

Now, I would go home to find Alexis Tayloe, still awake, expecting to be fucked, dressed like some middle-Europe dowager in some extravagant ball gown, which I would then laboriously take off her and leave in a bejeweled puddle on the floor, while we made desultory love, emotionless, sex-less, which makes it hard if you're the man, particularly if you've been doing cocaine for seven hours. But I was twenty-eight. I rose to the challenge and made listless love to this dying woman with large, fleshy breasts and a grow-ing pile of ball gowns on my floor, crawled over by rats in the night.

It is very hard, when you're on top of a woman with breast cancer, not to feel her breasts for lumps. I found noth-ing, but then I didn't really know what I was looking for, and then we would sleep and I would wake at five to find her in my fucking bathrobe, her ample body spilling out of the terry cloth, *my* goddamned bathrobe, her flat, broad, bare feet on my filthy floor, and we would be off to work, I to The Firm, she to her radiation therapist at Mt. Sinai and then to her personal shopper, Mrs. Selma LePage, at Saks Fifth Avenue. Death and its approach gives you both an enormous amount of energy and a total disregard for going into debt, as the victims of the coming plague were to find out in a very short while. But this was before the plague, when everybody was having unprotected sex with any living being who happened to be there when your dick got hard.

And with Alexis, the day ended the same way, every day. I would pull up to my nearly derelict building, enjoy, for a moment, the rich smells of the Spanish restaurant, climb up past the whorehouse, watching the johns leave with their furtive glances, and on up to Hovel Hall, where I would find Alexis waiting in another, more elaborate ball gown. I asked her why she was buying so many.

"Oh, Cyril is always dragging me to some function or other. Charity things. Biafran children. Unwed mothers. I need to look the part of the politician's wife." One could only imagine the yawn factor involved in going to something called a function with Cyril, whom I had met once, and whom I found to be the human equivalent of landfill.

This went on for eleven days. Eleven days, eleven radiation treatments, which I began to suspect never actually took place, eleven ball gowns, at least $100,000 worth, the alleged lump in her breast that had either gotten smaller or not, if it ever existed at all.

I had made love to Alexis Tayloe eleven times, like a good boy, the perfect host. During the sessions, she lay there motionless and bored, almost so uninvolved that she found it difficult even to spread her legs. A woman can simply lie there and think of the mother country. A man has a rougher time when it comes to sex without desire. An erection is required. But I somehow found the thought of Alexis Tayloe's imminent death, God forgive me, to be intensely erotic, so I made love to her as a necrophiliac dreams of corpses.

The last morning, shaved and showered in an effort to wash Alexis Tayloe's smell off of my skin, I said my awkward good-bye, managing to do so without kissing her lips.

She said, "You never paid me back the thousand dollars you owe me. So I figure it would have cost me at least a hundred dollars a night to stay in a hotel, so I'm considering the loan paid back, since I've been here eleven nights."

It took a lot to shock me in those days, or to hurt my feelings, since I had so few genuine feelings anyway, but I was appalled. I said, "Well, if you were hiring me as a rent boy, I would have thought the going rate was either nothing at all, or a good deal more than ninety dollars a night. Good-bye."

With a sigh of relief I closed the door behind me, and when I came home that night, drunk at two a.m., she was gone without a trace except for the price tags from the ball gowns, which littered the floor, in an effort, undoubtedly, to fool the customs people in England into thinking that she always traveled with eleven brand-new ball gowns.

That was it. Alexis Tayloe was gone, and I was never to know whether or not the cancer was real, whether, if it was real, she had survived, whether Cyril ever got into Parliament, whether Olympia ever stopped getting a rash every time her mother picked her up.

There was only this: at Christmas, a card arrived, with

Cyril and Alexis Tayloe printed on the inside with some vague nonreligious wishes for a happy holiday season, so it must have been the card they sent out to Cyril's supporters, people they didn't really know. The stamp on the card had a picture of the Queen of England on it.

At the bottom of the card, there was this note: "I can't tell you how many ways I would like to hurt you. I can't express how may ways I would like to cut you to the quick."

It's hard to talk about the eighties without using the word "fucking" a lot, since I spent a great deal of my time either in a rage or seeking out someone to have sex with me, or both simultaneously, even though it's a word I rarely if ever use now.

When I looked at Alexis Tayloe's printed Christmas card, not even engraved, merely printed, I thought, *So much for fucking hospitality. Fuck you, Alexis. Fuck your breast cancer. Fuck your fucking dresses. Fuck you and the horse you rode in on.*

And then I never thought about her again, except at Christmas when the cards would come in, although never again from Alexis Tayloe.

Luckily, almost nobody sends Christmas cards anymore.

CHAPTER TWELVE

The Do's and Don'ts
of Rising and Falling

❖ ❖ ❖

We used to play a game called Misery Poker. The greatest bartender in the world, Shirts, so called because he had been literally known to give the shirt off his back to some hopelessly drunk twenty-four-year-old who had puked all over his Turnbull & Asser shirt, would be the judge, the final arbiter. He presided behind the bar at the rundown place that was closest to The Firm, Callaway's, and was always waiting with a smile and a Tanqueray at two a.m., which is when we often reluctantly hung up the phone for the night. He'd listened to so many horror stories about selling and trading, about the terrors of the first years, that he could have been one of us.

The game was simple. If your workload was a bigger nightmare than any of your colleagues', you got to drink for free all night. "I've pulled four all-nighters in a row." "I'm staffed on three deals, and I haven't seen daylight since Easter." It was taken for granted that you would lie and embellish, to gain sympathy and get free drinks. Not that we needed anything for free, but drinking without paying felt like a mother's soothing touch on your sick brow. How we loved it. Our misery. We ate and drank the rigors of our chosen profession, the road to ultimate riches stretching straight ahead of us, littered with land mines of misery. We had T-shirts printed up, emblazoned with The Firm's logo on the front, and the slogan WE EAT OUR YOUNG printed in bold letters on the back. It was the Superbowl of hard jobs, which is why we put up with the shit, because, if you survived, the rewards were tangibly enormous. Our greatest goal was to invoke fear in the hearts of colleagues and clients alike. And we thrived on it.

Except not everybody thrived. Two guys died in the same month in 1984, marking clearly where at least some of the land mines lay. Both deaths were tragic, of course, but each was also irritating, creating a caesura of silence and schadenfreude in the otherwise unblemished culture of success. I mean, somebody dies, for God's sake, you have to stop betting against oil futures in Dubai for at least a few minutes, by which time the whole canvas of the world's economy may have changed, leaving you no longer in the picture.

Conti went first. Nobody knew his first name, or, if we had, we had forgotten it. Peter, the obituary in the *Wall Street Journal* said. He was twenty-two, an intern, and a true shark. He had moved a cot into the boiler room so that he didn't have to commute to work. See, we were all brilliant. We all worked like dogs. The only way to distinguish yourself your first year was to work harder than anybody else, in Conti's case, to work yourself literally to death.

So, Conti slept in the boiler room, and never saw the light of day. One afternoon, after pulling six all-nighters in a row, his heart blew up while he stood at his desk, on the phone. His heart blew up and killed him dead, at twenty-two.

EMS was called, and he was pronounced dead and wheeled off the floor on a gurney with hardly a pause in the action.

The next day, though, there was a minute of silence to mark his death. Even the Big Guy came down and said a few sympathetic words about what a good candidate he had been, made of the stuff The Firm expected and demanded, the energy, the enthusiasm, the brilliance. It was obvious the Big Guy wouldn't have known him if he'd run over him in his Bentley, but still, a death is a death, and we waited out the full minute in silence, well, not exactly silence, since the phones didn't stop ringing for a second, and our fingers were itching in our pants to answer them. So passeth Peter Conti.

After he died, the winner of the nightly game of Misery Poker was always called Conti, probably still is, even though the reason for the name has no doubt long since been lost in the speed and click of the rolling dice.

The second death was even more shocking: Harrison Wheaton Seacroft IV, who we called Helter Skelter because of the aggressiveness of his attack mechanism. A true pit bull. He was a big guy, a rugby player, and nobody's voice was louder. When Helter Skelter made a deal, everybody knew it instantly by the roar he bellowed across the floor.

We had been sort of friends. I had spent a weekend with his family at their huge pile in Southampton the summer before, a house not bought, just one of those things that was "in the family." I met his parents, nice people who did things with the kind of elegant simplicity that is only bought with a great deal of very old, very honorable money. His father had a seat on the Exchange.

There were lawns, immaculately groomed, a discreet pool that couldn't be seen from the house—too vulgar. Servants who unpacked your suitcase for you. Lunch beneath a big tent on the lawn served by women who had been with the family since before I was born, seemingly before time began. Dinner at eight thirty, dressed appropriately in sherbet-colored linens, a light cashmere sweater when the chilly breezes sprang up from the ocean so that candles flickered and danced as they had at this same table in this same gazebo for four generations of Seacrofts. One could feel the genial ghosts of all the Seacrofts sitting at the head of the table, barefoot in pastel linen, a life in which far more is saved than is ever lost.

He believed that credit cards, which had been invented in his lifetime, were the doing of the devil, the scourge of the middle classes. He didn't believe in debt. He felt that if you couldn't afford something, you simply didn't buy it, although the old boy was so rich it was a rule that rarely had to be invoked. They had the largest Manet still in private hands hanging in the library of their summer house. Harrison was heir to all this, and was rapidly building his own place at the family table.

He had been two years on the trading floor already and, at twenty-eight, was richer than most people dream of being, ever. Their minds just don't count that high. He was looking at retirement at thirty-two. And he killed himself. He got a phone call, a private phone call, an almost unheard-of occurrence, but one that caused him to leave his station on the floor and take it in his private office, white carpeting, a Richard Prince on the wall. It was all clicking into place for him, and then he got this call, which lasted no more than thirty seconds, and then he wrote a short note and addressed it to his parents.

He came out onto the floor and sought me out and shook my hand, curiously, and then handed me the note and asked me to see that his parents got it, by hand, not by mail. On the bottom left of the envelope, he had written, "kindness of . . ." and then my name, and I took the letter, not knowing what was going on, and I watched as he went back into his office. I saw it all, while nobody else even raised a head to watch as he did what he did.

He took off his shoes and placed them neatly under his desk, picked up a fire extinguisher and slammed it through the plate glass window of his office, killing two people on the street below, and then he jumped out the window, and fell seventeen floors, roaring as though he had just made the biggest trade of his life, which I guess he had, to land on the roof of one of the waiting black cars. The rest of the guys on the floor didn't even notice his absence until the cops showed up later. Somebody picked up the phone still lying off the hook on his desk, a man in Zurich still screaming as though nothing had interrupted the urgency of the deal that was taking place, and we gently cradled the phone on the receiver. End of deal. End of Helter Skelter Seacroft IV.

This was obviously not supposed to happen. Ours was a life of continual advancement. Failure and weakness were not allowed. It's one thing to have your heart explode at the age of twenty-two, it's another thing to jump out the window with $13 million in the bank.

Of course, we all put on dark suits and went to the funeral, looking appropriately stark, the wake and the funerals held necessarily at night, since nobody would be fool enough to think we would leave the trading floor before seven o'clock, but we knew in our hearts that he and Conti were both losers.

After the funeral, at the small reception at the Colony Club, his mother came up to me. Nobody had known who to invite since nobody had known who Helter Skelter's friends were, even his parents, who claimed that I was the only friend of his they had ever met, my entrée being good lineage in an old Southern family. We noticed that his father had not attended the funeral.

His mother took my elbow, "Come sit with me for a minute," and we tucked ourselves into a quiet corner and sat on the edge of two gilt chairs, ridiculously fragile, Mrs. Seacroft in a stark and perfect black suit with a single strand of pearls at her throat, her face drained of color, awash with grief and loss. He was their only son, out of five children.

"His father wouldn't come. He was outraged, and says

he's washed H Four from his memory forever. He says there is no forgiveness. Mothers are different."

She paused. She didn't know where to go next.

"He had the disease. That cancer. He was a homosexual. I can't even say it. It's unbearable to think of. He had everything. Girls adored him. I loved him with all my heart, my first child and my only son. How could he do this to me, to us? Why didn't you tell us?"

"I had no idea. I swear I didn't."

"That he could bring this shame into our house. That's what his father will never forgive. He would not, he will not, have a son who was, who was . . . that way."

"He was a nice man. A lovely guy."

"He was a liar. He chose to destroy us, not even by jumping out the window, but by living that lifestyle, by lying to us about who he was, because he knew we would never ever accept it. If he hadn't jumped, he would have been without family, he would have died with nobody to hold his hand, to give him the slightest comfort."

"It wasn't his fault. I would have held his hand."

Suddenly vehement, she flashed her icy eyes at me. "Of course it was his fault. Do you think we did anything to . . . to . . . make him that way?"

"God made him that way."

"And God punished him. His father won't allow him to

be buried in the family plot, where we have all been buried for four generations. His name is never to be spoken again. We've thrown out every picture of him. We've burned the clothes hanging in his closet. We could catch it from his clothes. I had two children born dead. I wish he had been one of them. I recovered from those deaths, I went on, because that is what you do. This, this . . . I will never get over it. I am just as infected as he was." Her voice rose to a pitch of anger I could not have imagined in her. "He ate off of our china. He slept in my sheets. I will burn every one of them." And she started crying, wracked with sobs. I put my hand on her shoulder, she shrugged it off violently. She pulled herself together and said calmly, "I'm sorry. I shouldn't have said anything. I should have taken it to the grave. But there was nobody else.

"He was my boy. My only son. And he was a liar, and a deviant, a disgrace. I will never be happy again. Could you leave me now? There are hands to shake. Appearances will be kept up. The grieving mother, bravely taking in the death of her beloved son. A lie, all of it, but it must be done. Good-bye. You're welcome to visit us at any time." The words were spoken without the slightest conviction.

I walked home. Helter Skelter a queer. He jumped because he had just been given a death sentence, and because he couldn't let the world know how he had gotten ill. And

I thought of all those nights in all those clubs, the dark bathrooms where men and women mingled high on drugs, grabbing for whatever skin there was, fucking any orifice that was offered. My face flushed with shame. What if? What if I was going to get the same phone call one day soon? I still insisted to myself that I was not a homosexual, but there was no denying I had done the things Harrison had done.

God help me, in those bathrooms, in the balcony at Studio, I had fucked men and I had enjoyed it. I was infected, and suddenly the streets were filled with men who were infected, too, just like me. We were all dying. All walking through the night, in dark clubs and alleys, high on coke and meth and Quaaludes and smack and flesh. Highest of all on flesh. And for that we would die. For the sweetness, the loveliness of touch, the feel of skin against your own, we were all to die.

We couldn't stop and we couldn't go back.

Harrison IV. HIV. A martyr to love. Riding the express train to being banker-splat on the top of a car that would have taken him home and into the night where he could not, would not live lying about the sex between his legs and in his heart.

Dying for love, that kindest of emotions. Pause for a minute and weep on 24th and 7th, surrounded by brooding, handsome boys in leather jackets, in muscle shirts, all those young men, all around. Me.

Maybe I had missed the bullet, but I didn't think so. I didn't deserve it. I would wake in the morning with the same hungers, and the party, although it was over and had turned lethal, the party would never stop and I would play until it killed me.

Dying. Dying for love. God help us.

The wages of skin is death.

In the morning, I felt as though my mood of last night was foolish. I felt invincible, despite the half gallon of vodka I had drunk when I had gotten home. The liquor had washed me clean. I *was* invincible and nothing would kill me, certainly not a few drunken moments in the dark at Steve Rubell's House of Sin.

After all, at twenty-eight, what's a little bad behavior? I was just being maudlin. In the light of day, it all seemed foolish. Seacroft was unlucky. The streets would not be piled with corpses. It was an age in which bad behavior was not only allowed, but encouraged and rewarded.

Up to a point. Bellowing like a bull in heat was encouraged. But certain things just weren't done at The Firm, and we learned them in our very first years.

Do not dress better than your boss.

Do not get drunker than your boss.

Never insult a client, no matter how stupid or rude they are. After all, these are people who have the requisite $20 million in cash it took to open an account at The Firm, and the one thing that was to be respected, above all else, was money—and the people who had it.

Come to work neat and pressed like a fine pair of sheets. But if you didn't look rumpled by nine a.m., you weren't working hard enough. Tie undone, sleeves rolled up, shirttails hanging out of your pants. A sartorial wreck, but with the ruddy glow of victory on your face.

A horrible apartment at a good address is better than a great apartment at a bad one.

Never wear an Hermès tie. Leave those to the lawyers and golfers.

Never be daunted in public. If failure comes your way, if a deal goes south, walk away as though you had nothing to do with it.

If your boss gives you a Mont Blanc pen at the end of a salary negotiation, you've just been taken to the cleaners.

Do not die before forty. Never, ever kill yourself. Even if, like Helter Skelter, you have the good sense to leave a $1,000 pair of shoes neatly under your desk. After he died, nobody would touch the shoes. The security people were left to clean out his personal effects, photographs of his parents, his siblings, a man none of us knew, but even they wouldn't touch his shoes. They sat there for days until one day they were mysteriously gone. They lasted longer than the memory of Seaforth himself.

If one of your colleagues is fired, never speak to him again. If you pass him on the street, or sit next to him at a football game, do not acknowledge him. Failure is catching. All your friendships on the floor are purely circumstantial, contextual, and vanish when your colleague is marched out the door, his phones shut off, carrying his pitiful box of personal items accompanied by a security guard. If you continue to hang out with him, you will be tainted with failure yourself, a scent of doom that will never wash off.

Never wear cheap shoes. And, when you get a pair of new shoes, polish them twenty times before you wear them on the street. Your shoes should look, not like you bought them, but like you inherited them from a rich uncle.

Never get a cheap haircut.

Never let your heart blow up at your desk. It shows excessive zeal.

Never never never. Always always always.

The culture of success marches on, and you better stay in step or step out of the way because you will get flattened.

I got flattened. But, I have to say in my defense, I went out like a man. I flattened myself.

CHAPTER THIRTEEN

Trotmeier Takes a Drive

❖   ❖   ❖

L ouis Patterson Trotmeier came up with me. He won the poker thing. It wasn't always the same poker thing—the old man changed it every time so people couldn't pass the answers along. Louis's was a single hand of Five-card Stud.

Louis had jacks and fours. No telling what the old man had. The old man drew two cards, and Louis knew the man across the desk wasn't drawing two cards to fill a pat hand. He wasn't just holding a pair and a kicker. So Louis threw in his pair of fours, and drew three cards. One was a jack.

Louis laid his hand on the table. The big man across the desk just folded his cards and threw them on the desk.

Louis looked him in the eye. "Sir. The odds of drawing a full house after being dealt two pairs of anything are 7.7 to 1. If you had had three of a kind, your odds of drawing a full house are 10.7 to 1. I figured the numbers were on my side. Sir."

"You're a numbers guy."

"Crunch the numbers then play by your gut. Numbers don't tell you what's going to happen. They just give you an opportunity. I'm a numbers guy with balls. I play the hard hunch, and what did I have to lose? There are other places to work."

He started the next day. His specialty was going with the informed hunch, and it took him very far very fast.

We called him Louie. He had the looks of a verifiable Greek God. A long, aquiline nose, a perfect body after hours and years at the Sports Training Institute, and a machismo that needed no verification. Louie colored his hair, the only man I have ever known to do such a thing, and his delicate but undeniably masculine features were corona-ed by golden curls cut by Frederic Fekkai himself. I have never seen a man more beautiful, even when he was sitting in the chair with squares of Reynolds Wrap all over his head.

He was a great trader; face it, he was flawless at everything, flawless, and he ran through a string of girlfriends that impressed not only his friends but occasionally the papers as well. Trading bored him, sex did not, and so he was even better at sexual conquest than he was at trading, and he was, as I said, a damned fine trader.

Another thing he had brought with him from generations of Trotmeiers on The Street, something not one other person we knew had the least inkling of, was how to save money. The day he got his job, he went to a bank, opened an account, and borrowed a thousand dollars and put it away somewhere where even he couldn't get it. Then he paid it off. Then he borrowed five thousand dollars, and so on, forever, even though he began making ridiculous amounts of money, while the rest of us were living like the tsars, going to restaurants like Frank's—a meatpacking district legend where Fat Frank presided, under an enormous portrait of himself, from two a.m. until seven, serving fried eggs and beer and bacon to the butchers who hung out there, and then turning it over to his son who ran the lunch crowd, and then the dinner crowd, serving up four-inch sirloins that made you scream with desire, Bloody Marys so high in alcohol that you could see through them—as Fanelli said, "If you can't see through them they're not doing their job"—and martinis that looked like they'd been made by Fabergé, at prices that made your hair stand on end. There was a great, late-night period of crossover, when the boozers and beefers were still sucking back $400 bottles of Pomerol, as the butchers, their hair still slick from the shower, still wiping the sleep from their eyes, began to roll in for breakfast before work at two. The street outside was filthy, everything was filthy in New York in those days, garbage everywhere, used needles, rats the size of watermelons, but Frank's was particularly filthy out on the sidewalk, since the whole street was covered with meat scraps and rats and tranny hookers leaning in the windows of the stretches and telling drunk traders that they, the trannies, knew exactly what they, the boozed-up bankers, *really* wanted, right more often than not, so the stretches circled the block, the windows steamed with fellatio and pot smoke until the sun was well up.

Overpriced food and bad service were the main virtues of the restaurants we liked, that and room for the limos to wait.

God, Frank's was great on bonus day, when we ran up $3,000 wine bills, smoking $400 illegal cigars, rolled by hand on Cuban thighs.

Trotmeier stayed on in his first apartment on Twenty-Third Street, where the rent was an astonishing $575 a month, not that it didn't show, an apartment so foul we called it Roach's Revenge, through the doors of which passed, nightly, the most beautiful, glamorous, completely fucking deliriously luscious girls in New York. He did not give these girls Birkin bags from Hermès or square-cut yellow diamonds at Christmas. He gave nothing but the eloquence of his youth and good looks and his ostensibly gigantic willie. He was a millionaire several times over by the time he was twenty-five.

Trotmeier would live with each of these girls for some weeks or months, even a year here and there, and the parting was never rancorous. He was not the kind who went around writing his phone number on girls' tits in nightclubs. He was, as they say, a gentleman. The affairs would always end with the same bittersweet regret, and he truly loved every one of them. He loved the way they smelled, and the glide of their tender skin, and he loved their conversation, always so bright with promise. He left not one of them worse off for wear, and they would always remember that he was not one of the bad ones.

His great-grandfather had been on The Street before the century turned, and every man in his family had made his living the same way, so they were a kind of royalty, although he was as much a flâneur as anybody, relentlessly social, at the Mudd Club or Area or Reno Sweeney every night, glorious girls on his arm, eating in all the best restaurants, attracting other rich, famous people to him, like Vitas Gerulaitis, who gave him tennis lessons. But he never, not for one minute, took his eye off the meter. He intended to be done with work by the time he was thirty, and he was well on his way. He was also one of the kindest people I have ever known.

Then Susanne Leiber came into the picture. She was from California, pretty although not the prettiest, but she had something. She was a brightness on her way to a greater brightness. She designed fabulously expensive jewelry for an iconic store on Fifth Avenue, so she worked, and she was wide awake from the minute her lustrous dark eyes opened. Trotmeier fell hard for her, although Trotmeier fell hard for them every time. Sometimes he would watch a girl walk through the door of a bar and say, "Oops, here comes my next mistake." At any rate, he fell, and it wasn't long before she had packed her loupe and whatever else and moved into Roach's Revenge.

So, for Trotmeier, there was at least the promise of connubial bliss. He went out less. Susanne and Louie gave dinner parties in his wreck of an apartment, four flights up, beef tenderloin and micro greens catered by the best in town. And Mrs. Trotmeier descended, the first time she had ever set foot in Roach's Revenge, and her general disappointment in Louie's choice of abode was instant and almost overwhelming. She declared the place unlivable, and proceeded to dismiss and discard all of Louie's furniture, the ratty futons, the cheap mattress on cinder blocks, the tatty rugs, all of it, replacing it with down sofas and Persian rugs and curtains from Clarence House and real china.

More important, she brought along Lenny the Exterminator, who took one step inside the door, breathed deeply, and

announced, "You have a serious infestation problem here."
And she brought along Loretta—"She's just like family"—
whose job was what it always had been, to clean the Trotmeier's houses, down to running a toothbrush through the
cracks between the floorboards.

In the end, it looked like an English chintz and Chesterfield sofa country house trapped inside a dark, decaying,
rat-infested shoebox. Which, I guess, is what most English
country houses actually are like.

So everything was all set. The future clear as crystal.
The royal couple, the perfect pair. Mrs. Trotmeier was ready
just to call Saint Laurent for the dress, book the Colony
Club, and get the damned thing over with, and Susanne
and Louie were not averse to this idea. Susanne wanted to
walk the vastly long aisle at St. Bartholomew's, where every
Trotmeier had been married since 1897, bridesmaids and
flower girls scattered before her like confetti on New Year's
Eve. Susanne wanted a baby. Louie did, too, strangely. Our
golden Louie, the first to fall.

Susanne flew home to consult with her mother in California. There didn't seem to be a father. DYK. In this case
the "D" meant either Dead or Divorced, but in any case his
absence was hardly noted.

Even with Susanne away, Louie stayed away pretty much
from the night scene, eating Japanese takeout at the Duncan
Phyfe table his mother had installed.

One night, a bitterly cold night in the winter, Louie was in bed at 12:30 when the phone beside his bed rang. It was Vitas on the other end.

"Get up, take a shower, dress nice, and be downstairs in front of your door in half an hour."

"I'm asleep."

"Wake the hell up. I have a surprise for you. I'm sending the car."

"Vitas, you're evil."

"*Semper paratus*, baby. *Semper paratus.*"

This story is true. It really happened. Most of the stories you hear about the eighties in New York really happened, like the woman who took the windows out of her tenth-story apartment so she could get a crane to raise a fifteen-foot Christmas tree up and through them and into her cavernous living room. That really happened, too. I don't think many things like that happen now. Maybe they do. Not my street anymore, as they say.

Anyway, one o'clock found Louis standing on the street corner, under the light, in a fine cold mist, his golden mane sparkling. Gray slacks, Oxford button-down and a cashmere blazer with horn buttons, never brass. The Trotmeiers didn't believe in overcoats, whatever the weather, except for funerals, and then only black Chesterfields from H. Huntsman and Sons in London, some of which were generational, having passed from father to son.

So the rain, the mist really, of a winter's night, was backlit and Vitus's yellow Rolls-Royce pulled around the corner, and the driver, who spent his days stringing rackets for Vitas, got out and smartly opened the door and a long arm shot out into the cold night and the hand at the end of the arm was holding a glass of brandy. Can you see it clearly? Can you see it now? Louie could, and he, drawing a short breath and thinking of Susanne one last time, sitting now with her mother in California talking about tulle and *peau de soie,* probably, and that long walk down the aisle at St. Bartholomew's, stretched out his own hand, took the brandy and drank it down in one gulp, and got into the back of the car, the door closing noiselessly. The hand belonged to an arm that was attached to a woman who was the current queen of pop divas, a creature so magnificent she had only one name.

"Hiya, baby," she said. She was wearing something in the winter night that was practically nothing, and she pulled Louie forward with her long arm and kissed him and she could taste the brandy on his breath, and then she pulled back and said, "Hiya, baby," again, which was practically all she said or ever needed to say.

The Diva's "Hiya, baby" changed the game forever for Louis Paterson Trotmeier. The panther, the stalking carnivore in him, long caged, was at large and on the prowl, and he looked at the Diva and he said, "Hiya," back, shyly, and then he devoured her whole, at one gulp, like an oyster shooter in a Mexican bar.

That night, in her vast suite at the Sherry Netherland, where she was staying at huge cost, in the darkness of a bedroom, in a bed on which the sheets were so fine, so crisp, you might have written your will on them, the Diva was everything to Louie. She was not a woman, she was a world, her white skin like a vast desert over which he swooped, touching down here and there, the dry places and the moist, the oasis where he drank himself into life.

Trotmeier, his patrician body worked to perfection, learned that, until that night, he had known nothing about women, about how to please them and how they could give pleasure in return. The Diva gave Trotmeier an all-access pass into her life and her body, took Trotmeier into her arms, and it was not just great, it was wonderful, and it changed Louie's life forever.

During a pause, he said to her, "Baby. I live with a woman. I love her and we're probably getting married. So whatever happens between you and me has to stay absolutely secret. Secret to the grave. Promise?" And the Diva promised, crossing her heart where a small gold cross glittered in the night, and then proceeded to fuck the brains out of Trotmeier until the swallows woke on the windowsill with the rising sun, and Louie had to go to work where he promptly told me and several others that he had made love to this tabloid headline, this total creation of sequins and sex, and the Diva, after a long and peaceful nap, got on the phone with her publicist and told her everything.

It went on. Every night, they would go out adventuring in the night, her fame giving them instant access to every pleasure dome—straight, gay, rough, sleazy, elegant—that the vast city had to offer. Trotmeier no longer looked like the picture of health he had always been, not like the scion of one of New York's oldest and richest banking families. He looked, frankly, like a haggard wreck, and he had never been happier.

But, in New York, there are no secrets except terminal cancer, and word of the affair was bound to get out.

Young Susanne Leiber, in the checkout line at Ralph's in Los Angeles, glanced down at the tabloids, and there was Louie, on the cover, wrapped like a python around the almost naked Diva, at Xenon. She left her groceries in the cart, took the redeye that night, and packed up Louie Trotmeier like last night's dinner and threw him out with the trash and she never spoke to him or saw him ever again. So much for the long walk. She was, as I said, a brightness on her way to a greater brightness, and, in her world, there was no room for peccadillo or passion uncontrolled.

The Diva went out on tour. She gave Louie eight cashmere sweaters and a gold Rolex that said simply on the back, *Semper Paratus.* He never heard from her again.

Susanne went in to work and sobbed over her rubies and emeralds. Trotmeier sobered up and soldiered on, trying to act as if it never happened, knowing at the same time that his life had been changed irrevocably and that, should he outlive the Diva, the first thing he would think about when she died was a small gold cross glittering in the darkness at the Sherry-Netherland, and a girl, a bonfire of celebrity, saying "Hiya, baby," just to him and him alone.

One day, Susanne's boss, the man whose father's name was on the marquee of the iconic jewelry store, looked into the office and saw her in tears and asked what was the matter, and she told him the story, which he already knew, of course, and he asked her to come spend the weekend with him in Easthampton. Eight months later they were married, and that certainly raised some eyebrows around town. He was decades her senior; he was widely thought to be seriously gay, and here she was, just this nice, ordinary girl with pretty eyes and a somewhat weak chin from Los Angel*eees*.

"What does this *mean?*" Fanelli asked me over a cigar at Frank's, after hearing of the marriage.

"They love each other," I said.

"But what does that mean? He's gay."

"We know what it means, Fanelli. We just don't know what form it takes."

"Well, fuck me," said Fanelli. "This beats the hell out of everything."

They were the couple of the year, of the decade. They went everywhere arm in arm, with a kind of tenderness one rarely sees in any couple. They meant, for a time, the world to each other, which is the long way of explaining how little Susanne Leiber came, at an early age, to appear on the arm of an aging homosexual jeweler wearing a twenty-eight-carat diamond pendant that had once belonged to Queen Victoria. The stone had a name, the Star of something-or-other, and to that name was added Susanne's. Girls scrambled for imitations of it at Bloomingdale's.

They were married for almost exactly ten years, and the diamond went up at auction the year following the divorce. Everything was done with perfect grace and taste. Susanne said of the diamond, "It is my hope it will be given to a lucky woman, as it was in the past, as a gesture of love and worn often and proudly."

Why is it that, as we lose our loveliness, the sheen of youth, we lose possibility as well? We acquire, but more is vanished than is given, and nothing makes up for the loss of the swallows at the Sherry, or the Victoria diamond, or the nights at Area when your booted feet ground the glass phials of amyl nitrate into the dance floor. Too much is lost. Too much is gone, every day, and it never comes back. You cannot get there anymore, or you get there to find the house empty of furniture, the baby grand covered with a dust cloth, shrouded silence in empty rooms where you no longer live.

Trotmeier married a beautiful but dumb model and bought an enormous apartment at the San Remo, but, after two children, he found her one drunken night in bed in his own house with some handsome trainer from the gym, so there was no more of that, no caroling parties during the season at the San Remo. And then he married a nice, ordinary woman who made up for her lack of spark with almost nothing.

He was almost the last to go after I got fired and everything changed. He still called, losing luster every time we met, showing pictures of his children but never a picture of the wife. His kindness was genuine, but our friendship had to do with a certain time, a certain place, and that place was no longer available to either of us. He always paid for the drinks.

Maybe that era was like an ecosystem that cannot sustain itself, and watching it die is sad. It is a sad thing. A deadly virus was so deeply embedded in its DNA that the death of the decade was occurring even as it was at its most verdant, its most resplendently dazzlingly alive.

"I wish . . ." said Louie one night, picking up the check, pausing.

"You wish what, Louie?" One of the kindest men I have ever known.

"I wish it could have gone on. I know it couldn't, she was way, way too much for me, it would seem ridiculous now, but, still, I wish. It makes my dick hard to think about it."

Such a sweet man, more than half his life gone now. Children grown. His drab wife always at home. And the ropes up at every club, clubs filled with identical children. The sons and daughters of the Trotmeiers of the world, going out into the night at fourteen, their eyes smeared with mascara.

"It had to end, Louie. It would have killed you."

"Then . . ." he said, picking up the change and overtipping as he always did. The laughing stopped. "Then I would have died happy. I would like to have died dancing with . . . I would like to have died. I think I would."

It was the last time I saw Louie. We left together, and we took off our gloves to shake hands in a falling snow. The flakes landed on his hair, and for a moment, it shone and sparkled again, a trick of the light. For a moment, in the light, and the breeze, Trotmeier was glorious again.

Like an angel.

CHAPTER FOURTEEN

Touching Strangers

❖ ❖ ❖

I'm the man on the other side of the glass. I see you, but you don't see me. You know I'm there, even as I watch you, but I am invisible to you. This is what it's become. I mean nothing to you, nothing at all.

If you happen to look into the glass, all you see there is your own reflection. But I want to say that I am there, beyond the reflection, on the other side of the glass where the ordinary people live.

I wear khaki pants and cotton and polyester plaid shirts and a tie. In the summer, I wear shortsleeved shirts. On each sleeve, the maker has cut a little V and put a button at its apex. I guess that's the decoration, the adornment that makes this shirt special, although the buttons usually fall off after about four trips to the laundry.

I wear nothing you would notice. Nothing that says there was ever a grandeur and a hubris about me. When my clothes get dirty, I take them in a blue nylon bag to the Chinese Wash 'N Fold, and they come back at the end of the day looking almost new. The people at the Wash 'N Fold lead simpler lives than I do, humbler, but they still manage to go home to Taiwan once a year, where for two weeks they live, with their American money, like kings and queens of yore.

I say things like "of yore" a lot. I say them to myself as I am watching you not watching me through the glass that I am forever on the other side of. I hate you, with your bustle and blare. You sit and talk of where to store furs and how to treat the hair, as Edna St. Vincent Millay said, of bright, new things, and people often laugh when you have finished speaking. You talk about not liking the latest bright thing as much as the *New York Times* did. You talk about not much caring for the food at the hot new restaurant in which you're currently having dinner. The noise, the din, of your conversation is appalling.

And, of course, you talk about money. Money is practically all anybody talks about these days. My mother taught me never to discuss money at the dinner table, but obviously we had different mothers.

You never talk about me. You detest the ordinary. You detest me. If thoughts of me somehow get into your brainwaves, they disturb the streaming thoughts of what a witty and wonderful life you're having.

I'm not having much of a life. It's not awful, just ordinary. I am trying to accommodate the memories of the life I had with the life I am now living, and I just can't do it. After being behind the wheel of a Lamborghini going 140 down Sunset Drive at four a.m., it's hard to get up and put on a polyester shirt and sell books at Barnes and Noble. But I'm not ashamed of it.

I walk with purpose, and leave almost no impression behind me. I sidle. I never rush. I walk four miles to work in the morning and four miles back, but I always allow plenty of time.

I am careful, on the street, not to jostle, not to be brushed against. I don't like the touch of strangers, not even the brush of a raincoat against my bare hand. I don't ask for much space in this world, so leave me in peace in the little I have.

I look at them, the other ordinary people, and they are not just meandering. They are like me, on their way to somewhere, and from somewhere, both so colorless that they barely even differentiate themselves in their minds.

I wear a nylon windbreaker most days, even when it's cold enough for an overcoat. The slick, cold nylon makes me feel like a dolphin cutting through cerulean waters in some place I will never again visit.

I have not, however, given up on life. I could speak to you. I could join the conversation. I have a 401K and I read all the time, so I know an awful lot about a shitload of things, things that would amuse you, that would make you laugh with delight when I finished talking. I could order with sophistication in any restaurant in the world. I can recite the St. Crispin's Day Speech. I know more about money than you could dream of.

I have had adventures. My life is not without event. I could tell you anecdotes.

For instance, decades ago, when I lived on my fellowship for a time in Florence, my life was so filled with adventure and event it was hard to tell when one thing ended and another began. I lived there for nine months.

On the afternoon of my last day, as I was packing up the dead remnants of what was meant to be a painting career, throwing them in the coal stove, a woman I knew named Sam dropped by and flatly said she wanted to have sex with me. Not now. Later. She was fortyish, tiny, a jazz musician with hair as red as her music was blue. I didn't know her very well, hardly at all, really. She wanted to come to my apartment late that night and spend my final night with me. The agreement was that she was to come at two, knock lightly, and I would let her in. The night often started at two a.m. in those days.

Sam was luscious, married, and twenty years older than I was. I offered to have sex right then, but she said, no, these things, her desires, needed time to blossom and that sex anticipated was far far better than sex on the fly.

That night, the night before I left, some English girls I knew, the unforgettably named Harriet Thistlethwaite, who had a younger brother named Cecil, and her roommates Rosemary and Prunella, gave me a going-away dinner party. It was filled with the kind of people who live on your side of the glass, but much younger. In your twenties, there is no glass, there is a breath of air where the windows would be, and the breath is so warm and welcoming that anybody could come in. There were all kinds of people at this party.

The English girls, all honorables, schoolgirls waiting for the term at Oxford to start, being waitresses in cafés and smoking like fiends, living on no money, were famous in their circle for a dessert they made out of fresh ricotta, instant espresso, and sugar and brandy. It didn't take much to distinguish yourself in those days. Everybody was young and bright and gifted, or they were beautiful, which trumped any hand on the table.

The food was spaghetti aglio olio, of course, it being the cheapest foodstuff you could throw together, the whole party probably costing about six dollars, helped by the fact that everybody brought two bottles of the cheapest wine. We didn't know. We reveled in what we had. The world had possibilities, limitless possibilities, and adventures, and food was of no importance and wine was cheap.

Cecil Thistlethwaite, who had been coming to Florence on his own since he was fourteen, to set off fireworks on January 27th, Mozart's birthday, on the very spot in the Piazza Signoria where Savanarola was burned to death, brought along a boatload of handsome and lissome friends. He introduced me to a guy named Tito, nice-looking, about my age, who, from the oversized calling card he gave me, was not only a count but was really named Parmigianino or Pontormo or something like that. We talked. *Tiziano.* That's it.

"Are you single?" Tito asked. I said I was.

"You don't have to be," he said in his Swiss boarding-school English. "I have a cousin. Lucia. Beautiful. Nineteen. She's looking for a boyfriend."

"I'm leaving in the morning."

"Stay."

"I'm sorry. It's impossible. I've run out of money." The fact that it was also bizarre, being asked to drop everything and live with a woman I'd never laid eyes on, didn't even occur to me. Remember, forty bottles of wine.

He moved on, but he'd circle back around every ten minutes or so, making the offer more enticing every time.

"She's very beautiful, Lucia. And she is very, very rich."

"Then why can't she get her own boyfriend?"

"She's very shy."

And later. "Lucia wants you so much."

"She's never even seen me."

"She watches you dance. At Mach Due . . ." which was a discoteque Harriet and I used to go to a lot.

"And she never says hello?"

"She's very shy, I told you. But she's in love with you."

"*Buggiardo,* it can't be true."

"Believe me or not. She knows what she wants."

Much later, almost thirty-eight bottles later and it was getting on and Sam was knocking at two, and I was ready to leave, he circled one more time.

"What's your favorite car?"

"The Ferrari Dino 246."

"She'll buy you one. Restored to perfection. She'll buy a big apartment with plenty of room for you, and all your clothes and food. And she'll pay you five thousand a month, just to spend."

"I have to go now, Tito. Tiziano. Someone is waiting for me. I'm sure your cousin is everything you say she is. I wish her every happiness."

"Her heart will be broken."

"I have to go. I have to go now."

"Do you mind if I walk out with you?"

So I said my many good-nights and farewells and promised lifelong allegiance and friendship to people I knew for certain I would never see again. I would be in classes at Wharton in three weeks and Florence would be very, very far away.

Tito and I left. The doors closed behind us and plunged us into pitch. It was one of those buildings where you had to hit a switch that turned on the lights for no more than twenty seconds, so you had to race down the slick marble steps to get to the street. Halfway down, the lights went out and everything turned to a vast blackness, a vast, slick blackness. We stopped on the landing, in front of an enormous two-story window that looked out, as our eyes grew accustomed to the dark, on the rising Tuscan landscape. Such a beauty.

"May I ask you a question? If you won't move to Rome with my cousin, would you come home with me and sleep with me tonight in my apartment?"

I was beyond drunk. Tito reached up and touched my cheek with the flat of his left palm. Half of his handsome face was in shadow.

His hand burned my face, and my blood ran suddenly

cold and I threw myself into the descending darkness, grasping for the banister, hoping for purchase on the eighteenth-century marble staircase. I ran all the way home, pausing to say farewell to the transsexual hookers outside the grand hotels along the Arno. So sophisticated they were, making their nightly *passagiata* around Santa Croce.

When I got to my apartment, I let myself in through the street door and locked it, then locked myself in my apartment, closing the shutters so the full moonlight slanted on the terrazzo floor. And I waited. I was sealed inside like Aida in her tomb, inaccessible, but I waited, and at a quarter after two, I could hear through the shutters a timid knock, or what sounded like a knock, on the street door. I didn't move, sitting alone in my chair in the dark apartment, striated by the slanting moonlight.

She didn't knock again. I sat until four, but there was no sound. In the morning, I took my bags to the train station and on to London, and then to America and business school and The Firm.

My night of passion, of desire. My anecdotal adventure. Well, not such an adventure after all. An adventure manqué. The sad, almost musical adventure of an ordinary man, held dear almost forty years later. Three people who wanted me in one night. The memory of three people who wanted me at all.

The point is, if I were on your side of the glass, I would not sit silently. Just the other day, when I was walking to work quite early, passing a bank, I heard a small chirping sound I couldn't identify. Normally I don't pause in my walk, but that day, I paused and realized that the beeping was coming from the cash machine on the side of a bank. I stepped closer to investigate.

In the slot, the slot where the money comes out, there were five brand-new $20 bills. There was no one on the street, not a soul in the gray chilly dawn, and I took the money and the beeping stopped. The machine went dark and silent again.

I can understand forgetting your card, leaving it in the slot until the machine devours it for your safety and security, but the money? The whole reason you went to the ATM in the first place? How drunk or stoned do you have to be to leave the money just sitting there?

All day I burned with paranoia. I was on camera taking a hundred bucks that didn't belong to me, and I was sure that, at any moment, federal agents would walk through the door of the bookstore and cart me away. I considered giving the money to charity, or dropping it in the offering box at a Catholic church, but I did nothing. I kept it in the pocket of my ordinary pants.

We might have laughed over this at dinner, you and I, as I paid for a round of drinks. We might have. In a long-ago day, a hundred bucks would have bought a gram of cocaine to get us through the night. For the second between the time I took the money and the time it went into my pocket, I was you, I was on your side of the glass, admiring a diamond brooch you inherited from your grandmother. I was there. I was there and now I'm not.

Here's where I am. This is my adventure. I sit in front of my laptop late at night and I buy things. I buy clothes. I buy shoes. I buy crystal wine decanters. There are many online boutiques where you can do this. There is no salesman to be disdainful, there is no glass curtain. There is only the best of everything and the clack of your fingers on the keys. I buy these things with my credit cards, which are stored securely in my profile on these sites. Nobody sees me sitting in my old bathrobe, fresh from the shower, eyes alight with wanting and remembrance.

Packages arrive. I note happily that they were packed with pride by Jeanette L. or Rhoda D., and I imagine these women, geniuses with tissue paper, getting my box ready for me in Dallas or London. These are elegantly wrapped boxes, the kind that used to litter the floor of my bedroom in the loft on Saturday afternoons. The clothes in these boxes are exquisite, made of materials that are brilliant to the touch, in colors that make the eyes go dim. Silk and cashmere. Sea Island cotton. Wool and angora. The cut of the clothes is masterful, so that the jackets hang softly on my shoulders, almost weightless, the trousers hold to my hips and thighs in an embrace like a kiss.

I put the clothes on, and for a second I am that person all over again. For a moment, I am the best-dressed man in the world. Lanvin and Givenchy and Saint Laurent and Bottega Veneta, the boutiques that line Madison Avenue and similar streets all over the globe. I order from New York. I order from Paris, Rome, and I step into my new clothes like a king.

I watch Ryan Gosling on the *Tonight* show, wearing a Donegal tweed suit, and it takes some doing, but, over the days, I call the *Tonight* show and find out who made the suit, and it arrives in a box and I put it on less than a week later. However, I do not, in my apartment, look like Ryan Gosling.

I walk around for a while, catching my reflection in every mirror. I am, for those moments, the emperor of my life.

Then I take off the clothes and fold them. I make sure that they are folded exactly as they were sent, as Rhoda or Jeanette would have liked, wrapped in silver tissue as though they had never been touched. I fill out the return slip. I know the code for every reason for these returns. DNF: Did Not Fit. CM: Changed My Mind. The package, when I am done, looks untouched, and chances are it will be on its way to you as soon as it is returned to the inventory in the store.

I lie in bed, in my sleeping costume, between the

exquisite sheets that are all that remain of a life I once lived. A life in which somebody once ironed my underclothes. Daniel Storto, the best glove maker in the world, has made me a pair of gloves, fawn-colored kid leather from a tracing of my hand. Riccardo Tisci has made me a tuxedo. John Lobb has sent a pair of monk strap shoes, from measurements they still have on file in London, from the old days. They don't care that they haven't heard from me in thirty years. They could make me a pair of shoes tomorrow if I were to ask, which I do not, will not ever again.

In the morning I get up and take my medications, Ativan and Buspar for anxiety. I take the packages to be returned and walk in my ordinary pants past all the shop windows filled with all the things I will never again possess.

I am cold in my windbreaker. The sheet of glass shields your life from mine.

I had dinner with you. You do not remember it.

I gave you christening presents that went lost or into storage. I gave myself to the world at breakneck speed. I gave you the monogram of my life, of my heart, and you never even opened the invitation.

I tell myself that this is all right, but I trudge through the day, eager for the moment when I open the new boxes and become, for five minutes or ten, one of those on your side of the glass, the king of the universe.

CHAPTER FIFTEEN

Coming Home to Roost

❖ ❖ ❖

The rise of cocaine usage in New York exactly paralleled the widespread proliferation of the cash machine, those blinking seducers. "Going to the Wall," we called it, and there quickly developed an entire protocol of behavior for how to do it in company. Never look at anybody else's screen. Never hoot if no cash was forthcoming. This last part did not ever, ever happen to me.

Previously, when dinner was over and all the money was gone, we would just head for home, get in the limo and glide back to our beds. With the advent of the ATM, there was never an end to cash and, instantly, never an end to the list of skinny guys in walkups one could call to pick up a gram or two.

Sometimes, a party would gather. On other, better nights, beautiful women and wonderful boys would follow me home in about equal measure, for lines on the mirror and up the nose and eighteen-year-old single malt down the throat and eventually, bed at dawn, our beautiful, naked bodies sliding softly against one another, powdery and dry. Death hung over us all, and sex was heaven, eros and thanatos in equal measure. There was, in the air, in the plague years, the sense of an ending, a rush to have it all before the dark door closed and the bouncer turned his back on you.

We'll sleep when we're old, we used to say, knowing that day would never come, never suspecting that our beautiful, sensual lives would be truncated before we had time to have children. We saved nothing, we spent, every day, all there was, not just the cash. All the freedom and the beauty and the sex and the blood in our veins was hot from the expenditure.

I had moved out of Hovel Hall, leaving every single thing behind in that horrible apartment, and moved into the House of Heaven, a five-thousand-square-foot loft in Soho with a roof garden, where I installed a lap pool, red tape coming out of my ears to get it, but nothing would stop me. Naturally though, like any New Yorker, I held on to the lease for the old apartment I intended never to see again. New Yorkers don't let go of a cheap piece of real estate until the coroner rips the paper from their cold, intestate fingers.

I said I would use it as an office on the weekends, but it was really there for my increasingly frequent meetings, meetings that were never put down in my book, except the time and a name and a phone number, in case I was ever found hacked to death and floating in the Hudson. These meetings were ultimately without meaning, but they engraved themselves on my heart, ineradicable. Where was I going? What was happening? I had neither the time nor the courage to ask, but the key to that apartment stayed shiny as ever from use.

I got drunk at lunch. It didn't even start to slow me down.

I did nine grams of coke in an average week.

I got laid about the same number of times.

I bought my loft, my space, at the height of the market, and hired Alan, who was the most brilliant interior designer of the day. He had done Keaton, Barkin—movie stars and rich people, and everybody wanted him and I got him because I never did not get what I wanted. That's all.

He took my $3-million loft and completely gutted it. I lived in ruins. For two years, I walked through the doors to the sight of dumpsters in every hallway. He took what had been a five-bedroom loft and turned it into a one-bedroom one in which there was not one soft surface. I loved him. He had absolute clarity and a gentle way and tweed jackets, and he had AIDS.

In the loft, I wandered the night, alone or coupled,

drunk always, until I began to realize that every single surface had corners that were too sharp. Granite. Formica. Marble. Sharp as razors.

So I went out and got some foam rubber and duct tape and covered every edge with a layer of protection, so that, when I fell—and I was going to fall—I was less likely to end up in the emergency room needing stitches. It was important, of paramount importance, that I look fresh in the mornings, and I did, not one hair out of place.

In the ruins of this unfinished loft, I married Carmela Mickelson Chase, whose mother was the fifth richest woman in America. I did not marry her because I was afraid of finding myself alone on the sere and pustulant desert of AIDS. I did not marry to try to cure some sexual confusion, that confusion producing in me the happiest feelings of euphoria I have ever known. I could have it all, all the touch points, and could juggle and hustle and wrassle and make millions and I would still not burn to the ground. I was, in the arms of those men and those women, indestructible and deathless and beautiful and free.

In a man, there is a spot just at the base of his throat, in the hollow of his neck, and, if you put your thumb there, you can feel the beat of his pulse, and know love ad infinitum. With a woman, that spot is the curve of skin between her rib cage and her hip bone, a slope of beauty unlike

anything else in the world. And both were equally compelling and both were absolutely necessary to me.

No. I married Carmela Mickelson Chase because she had
come up from Philadelphia for a dinner party I was holding
in the loft, served by white-coated waiters from Glorious
Foods, each a beauty, passing the canapé that turned New
York on its ear that year, a tiny new potato hollowed out
to hold a dab of crème fraîche and a dot of caviar. Carmela
dressed that night in real Paris couture, ruby and diamond
earrings, dark Irish hair and eyes, and she showed up at the
party with her present, two Russian saber dancers she had
met on the street, old men in Hussar dress who danced for
us and bowed and left.

Carmela, which was not by any stretch of the imagination her real name, her real name having died in the chill
night air of the sleeping porches at Miss Porter's, had come
to New York to go to the Ballet, the New York City Ballet,
and been brought to my ruin by a friend, an astonishingly
luminous girl, Berry Berenson, sister of the actress Marisa,
and who was later to die in the first plane to hit the World
Trade Tower. There are only six people, and sooner or later
we are all yesterday's newspaper.

Carmela had beautiful hands, and the most beautiful
skin you can imagine, and there was almost nothing that
came out of her mouth that was not filled with a charm I

thought had died for me forever. In the middle of dinner, discussing photography, which is what she spent her days doing, she held her hand up in a certain gesture, her small hand raised above the pink rack of lamb as though she were a child candling an egg, and I knew that I loved her, and she looked at me and we both knew that she would be spending the night with me in the loft.

I said to Anne Kennedy, who sat on my right, smoking, so beautifully photographed with her exquisite sister Mame by Robert Mapplethorpe, he soon to die of the thinning disease, famously photographed, two brilliant beauties staring wide-eyed at the camera, two sisters who had come from Connersville, Indiana, to be the kind of girls they had read about in *Vogue* and *The New Yorker*—I told this beautiful, thoughtful girl that I admired a mint-green silk blouse she was wearing.

She held her hands aloft, as though framing a window: "It's my favorite thing." She gently waved her arms. "I love the cut. I love the color." And that was the thing about Carmela. I loved the cut. I loved the color.

And I have never, since that moment, despite what happened, have never not loved her, not for one second. I have never said one unkind word about her. Not a single day passes that I don't think of Carmela, with the most abiding love I have ever had the joy to know. My one true love, my rock of affection that will remind me on the coldest night that love is a real, true thing, that it has a shape and a boundary, that it has a gesture that can win you over and hold you forever in its gentle grasp.

After every other guest had gone, Carmela and I were lying in bed, having made love for the first time as fondly and efficiently as a couple married for half a century, and she raised herself up on her elbow as my hand slid down the slope of her hip, and she said, "Look. I have something to say. Either this ends in two years with me having a baby or I walk out of the door right now."

I kissed her, tears springing to my eyes, hearing the last of the waiters still clearing the tables, and I promised her. I promised her she would have a baby, ten babies, that she would be mother of the year. And she would have been, would have mothered a child as she held the imagined egg, if I had kept that promise, which I did not, to my eternal shame.

Which I did not.

A week later, she had left her lover and her loft in Philadelphia, and was hanging her clothes in my closets.

Three days after this, she stood in the bathroom, *my* bathroom, brushing her teeth as I left for work, and said, "Honey, we're out of toothpaste, would you get some on the way home?" We. In a week we were "we."

That night, she threw my Knicks tickets into a handy

dumpster and took me to Lincoln Center to see Balanchine's *Serenade,* her favorite of her many favorite ballets, all by Balanchine.

At the theater, the house hushed, the gorgeous Sputnik lights rose into the heavens, and that red curtain opened with the sibillance I was to come to know as the breath of my life, and there, on a twilight stage, in costumes by Jean Lurçat of such a color and cut, pale gray sapphire, ethereal, so beautiful they caused a crater to be named after Balanchine on Mercury, there stood ten women, reaching for the heights, in identical positions, and, at the end of each slender left arm, there was Carmela's delicate tiny hand candling her egg.

How do we bear it, the beauty that memory holds for us? How does it not just carry us away into oblivion? How can we hold such beauty in our hearts, knowing all we ourselves have done to lessen that beauty, our sins of omission and commission, our inexactitudes, our false starts and false intentions, the promises made in cocaine and the dark, never to be fulfilled?

We go on, frenching the beans, letting one dog out the door as the other wants to come in, trying, trying so hard to find in our abject lives the sanctity of memory, that place where we live always in beauty and terror until we think our hearts can't stand it but they do. They do. They can. They can forever.

Carmela didn't really have to work at anything, what with the moneybags ma whose generous checks came every two weeks, but she did, and she was genuinely brilliant at it. She took pictures. She dressed her girlfriends in dresses from her mother's vast collection of couture, sparkly, ethereal constructions of cloth that would float rather than fall to the floor, a history of the brilliance of fashion in the decades after the war, and she photographed them, and then she locked herself in her darkroom with a pack of cigarettes, a darkroom Alan had squeezed in where one of our imaginary children was eventually to sleep, and she made pictures that were lustrously graceful and elegant. She did this all day every day, with the most ordinary girls, girls she met at lunch counters, waitresses and secretaries, aspiring rock singers, not a beauty among them. Then I would come home from work around nine, the girls gone, the darkroom locked for the night with her secret key, and sit down with friends to an exquisite dinner, made by Carmela, served on Tiffany china with Chrysanthemum knives and forks, on permanent loan from Carmela's mother, part of Carmela's allowance.

We didn't break things. We didn't look on our lives as frangible. We had energy and youth and money. We ingested our lives as smoothly as a line of cocaine.

Work on the loft continued, and Alan slowed and weakened. He sat next to me in the fading sun in the English bankers' chairs that were one of his hallmarks, watching as a $63,000 Lalique crystal chandelier we had dipped into bloodred automobile paint was wired and hung over the granite table.

"Can I hold your hand?" he asked.

I gave it to him, and he held it softly in his, his hand so thin, so light.

"I'm cold all the time," he said. "All the time."

This was the last conversation we ever had.

"I'm afraid," he said.

"I know, Alan. I can't tell you how sorry I am."

"I didn't catch it from who everybody thinks it is. It wasn't him. Tell everybody that."

"I promise."

"And don't sing anything from *A Chorus Line* at my memorial."

"Promise."

The next time I saw Alan, he was in a glass room at New York Hospital and I was wearing a surgical mask and a hazmat suit. That's how scared everybody was back then. Nobody knew anything.

He was gaunt, unrecognizable. He was so intubated, his only means of communication was to write on a pad of paper by his bed. In a shaky hand, he wrote a note and handed it to me. "It wasn't him."

I folded the note and put it in my pocket.

I wasn't there when he died. He had built for me a space that was the envy of everyone I knew, and then he died and stayed dead. The loft was a gleaming engine for entertaining and it was only as I got used to it, came to be at home in it, that I realized, with the bankers' chairs and the banquettes and the grand piano, there was no private space in the whole of the entire loft. There was no place to sit and read a magazine. It was designed to hold large numbers of people, bright, happy people who were not wearing hazmat suits.

The only private space was Carmela's darkroom, from which she would emerge at the end of every day with ten or twelve prints. She knew the work was good. It was she herself who was inadequate.

"You don't love me," she would say in the darkness.

"Of course I love you."

"Well then, you don't love me enough."

"And just how much would be enough? How would you know?"

"When you get there, I'll tell you," and she would turn away from me in the dark, and we would sleep without touching.

In the morning, she would bring me coffee in bed, and we would drink coffee and smoke, and look at the wall opposite the bed, where she had pinned dozens of photographs.

One day, after I had gone off to work, she took down all the pictures, put them in a brown paper shopping bag and walked with them down West Broadway and into Sonnabend, the best gallery on the street. She talked her way into seeing Ileana, Castelli's former wife, who presided in a wig and her regal obesity over some of the most exciting art being made in the city.

Carmela dumped the contents of her paper bag on the gallery's desk, and twenty minutes later Ileana had scheduled a show. September. The sweet spot. It wasn't luck. It was tenacity and brilliance. The tenacity of a deeply insecure person, like the mother who is, miraculously, able to lift the car off the baby.

The opening was a triumph, and she had nothing but future. There was a party afterward at our loft. Five hundred people came, including the homely waitresses and saxophonists who had posed for the pictures.

And, sometime during the party, Alan said good-bye to the world. We played the Albinoni adagio at the New York State Theater and sat silently through a slide show of Alan's best work. Keaton spoke. Bette Midler sang "I'll Be Seeing You." Eros and thanatos. Glamour and death. Sooner or later, some side would win, one side would prove stronger than the other, and Alan would be largely forgotten, in the way that the five hundred guests, so used to going to openings and book parties at the houses of people they didn't really know, would wake up the following morning and wonder, while the coffee dripped, exactly how they had spent the last evening.

CHAPTER SIXTEEN

Packing Up the Circus

❖ ❖ ❖

C armela divorced me by six o'clock on the day I
got fired. *Semper paratus.* We had been together
almost exactly two years. There was no issue, as I
had always known there wouldn't be.

The following morning, I walked into a Ferrari dealer-
ship and bought a $300,000 car, whose seats hurt my back.
I bought it in a rage and drove it in pain until it went for
pennies on the dollar in the great fire sale that my life was
to become.

Carmela got everything. I gave with an open hand until
there was nothing left but bare skin. I moved back into Hovel
Hall, painted it battleship gray, and roamed the nights with
the rats.

There was an unmistakable sense, no matter how perfectly the suits were pressed, that the tide was somehow turning, and I was helpless in the tidal pull.

Carmela had loved Solitaire, a game I had almost never played. Back at Hovel Hall, I sat on the floor every night, after coming back drunk and stoned from the clubs, and played game after game of Solitaire, an open bottle of gin by my side. I played until I passed out or the gin was all gone or it was time to go to work.

Slap. Slap. Slap. The cards endlessly went into their piles. I was in mourning.

Three months later, at five in the morning, I played a perfect hand of Solitaire, sitting on the grimy floor of the apartment where I had acted with such sexual profligacy, even as I lived with Carmela in one of the most beautiful lofts in the most exciting city in the world.

I played the hand out, all the cards falling into four neat and undeniable ranks, and then I put the cards away, and I never played again, and mourning was over.

But Carmela never ended, and Alan never ended; the red chandelier still hung in the darkened dining room, and nothing from those days was ever over.

CHAPTER SEVENTEEN

In the Grip

❖ ❖ ❖

Of such terrors and demons, we are. The bodies litter the streets on which we walk. They ride with you in taxis. They sing hymns with you in church. They are everywhere, the dying, and their names are the names that fill your Filofax, which you grip to your chest with the passion you used to feel in a lover's embrace. Every day, you cross off another name, and write in your calendar another memorial, another black suit, another eulogy, a reading from Millay, a song from *Chorus Line,* a pair of tap shoes and a red rose on some buffet table upstairs at the Russian Tea Room, still decorated for a Christmas long past.

It was 1984, the year the plague came out of hiding and

showed its fangs on every street corner, and fear ran not just in the veins of our infected friends, but in the streets, like blood beneath the guillotine. Don't share a dessert, don't sit next to a man who has cut himself shaving, the year, in fact, that razors were no longer to be found in gyms, the virus can live in a teardrop, so don't tell me you can't get it from a toilet seat, and there was only one thing it meant in that sentence, and that was death. God forbid you nicked your neck shaving. You would count the days until the wound had healed completely, taking that as a sign you were safe.

My first thought, every morning—God help and forgive me—when I thought of my fallen colleagues, was that there were fewer dogs to bite me in the ass on the way up the ladder. I remember that thought with shame almost every day, and there is no undoing it, and there is no one to forgive me. Certainly I can't forgive myself.

So many dead. So many funerals. People who had never needed a dark suit before, now finding themselves putting one on two or three times a week. So many mothers and fathers who found out that their sons were homosexuals only when they saw the hideous bruises on their handsome young faces. The gaunt young men, strong and eager just a summer before, shuffling the streets of the Village. A restaurant called Automatic Slim's, whose name became synonymous with the disease.

Those nights in the clubs, in the dark bathrooms, the nights of unbridled sex, were now coming back to tear a whole generation into shreds of paper, tiny announcements in the *Times*. "After a short illness . . ." So many dying with not one solitary soul at their bedsides. The riotous spending by men who knew that their debts would die with them.

> *Old men forget, yet all shall be forgot*
> *Yet he'll remember with advantages*
> *What feats he did that day*

. . . the feats of bravery and cowardice, of foolishness and fear, young men whose lives turned into a sea of sorrow in an instant, with the first cough, the first red blotch on their sweet skin, and nobody paid attention, nobody paid attention, and there wasn't even a test until 1985, so the only way to know you had it was to get it, the outward and visible sign of an inward and invisible death, the day the music died, to steal a phrase, and there couldn't be any sharing of glasses or toothbrushes, no kissing, that greatest of inventions of Western civilization, and still men went to the baths and roamed the halls naked until dawn, fucking anything that passed, often not caring, some actually longing to be stricken so as to join their brothers.

And I'll say this once, and not again, and then I'll lay out the cards and you tell me the answer. People say there's no such thing as bisexuality, that bisexuals are homosexuals who are too afraid to embrace who they really are, and I say those people are lying to you, because they can't admit in their drab lives that there are men in whom the sexual urge is so strong it can be triggered by many forms of beauty, I lived with women and I fucked men, always on top, always the aggressor, the dominator, and I have never been happier, and have been less happy since the day the roads diverged in a yellow wood and I chose the one less traveled by, and I was diminished because of that choice and long for the days when I would wake up with her in my arms and meet him for lunch at the Pierre. Lunch for $700, the beauty of touch at noon.

> *He that outlives this day, and comes safe home*
> *Will stand a tip-toe when the day is named*

. . . and he will say, "I was there. I bear witness and what do you do? You place ads online and meet men for five minutes in a cheap motel and call that love because you cannot, will not grow up, because in all the world you are denied the right to couple, because you would rather spit on yourself than be spat on by strangers in the street, strangers who hate you, who wish you dead."

> *Then will he strip his sleeve and show his scars*
> *And say, "These wounds I had on Crispin's Day,"*

Except the scars are invisible now, the cry of pain is muted by the noise of the world, the yackety yack of young men who march in parades half-naked to proclaim their solidarity, their mothers and fathers walking beside them, and the whole idea of gay rights has turned into something that says that two men are free to kiss and feel each other up in front of Tiffany's.

And being a homosexual has lost its hidden power, its intoxicating allure, because it has lost the vicious prison of its secrecy, and love is no longer made on the gallow's steps, but en plein air, with all the world to watch, and sensuality has been replaced by mere vulgarity, and we who are old and have lived through it, yes, strip our sleeves and show our scars to a world that does not watch and does not even care.

And you want to say to all those mincing, self-loathing queers filling the aisles at Barney's, "You think I'm old and useless and unattractive, and I am, but I'm here to tell you that I invented you, I allowed you to become the kind of man who drinks mojitos at the Standard in Palm Springs, to fill the clubs on Mykonos every night with shabby, sanitized versions of what we knew and made live because there was a burning in the blood, a burning for sex, that act which, regardless of reproductivity, creates life every time it is performed."

And, if I could recreate for you the sexuality, the unstoppable force of kissing in 1979, the compelling secrecy that was homosexual life, the cruelty that caused Helter Skelter to jump out the window upon hearing his own death sentence, in the years just before the war, the feeling of lying skin on skin, and tongue to tongue and cock to cock, you would reel from the power of it, as though you had been struck by a Taser. You could not handle it. You couldn't bear it.

We are unfit to teach children.

We are unfit to raise families, an oddity like a dog that walks on its hind legs.

We are the death of religion and the albatross around the neck of American politics.

We are the starving children wolfing down as much as we can at the table of American culture.

We are incapable of playing the romantic lead in a Hollywood movie.

We were once the love that dared not speak its name, and still we lay naked and tangled and sweaty, children huddled in the storm, so tender, so kind, so violently in love. Now we blare that love with bullhorns during the second act of *Tosca* and we have become as heartless as the rest of America, the most heartless country on the planet.

We have been bound with barbed wire and beaten to death, we have killed one another, because for all the marches and the banners and the drag queens on TV, while

Holly and Candy and Jackie are forgotten, we are still, as children, taught to loathe the thing that makes us who we are.

It is 1981. A sixteen-year-old Puerto Rican drag queen who calls herself Putassa walks into a room full of men in evening clothes and I say to a friend standing beside me, "Who is that creature?" so perfect in her loveliness, so graceful and charming and delicate, so unacceptable in every way outside this room, outside of this moment, and he says, "That is the most beautiful boy in New York," as the lights dim and Holly and Jackie in black sequins and boas descend a staircase singing "Broadway Baby" from *Follies*. And Putassa gets up the next morning and goes to her day job at Saks, modeling designer clothing for rich women to choose from, including a blue satin ball gown by Oscar de la Renta eventually bought by a slightly heavy woman from London named Alexis Tayloe, who, to this day, wishes she had found more effective ways of cutting me to the quick, after I had expertly fucked her for eleven nights in a row.

But, people will tell you, look how much better things are now than they were then. Equal rights, equal protection under the law. You can GET MARRIED!!! And those same people leave Matthew Shephard to rot in a ditch in Montana, and feel squeamish when two female lawyers with two children move in next door, liberals on the Upper West Side who snicker behind their hands when two men walk by with a Vietnamese baby in a stroller. Two successful young men turning a slant-eyed baby into a queer.

And I, who could find nothing but self-loathing on either side of the Rubicon because what I wanted was both, because I wanted it all, and that is not allowed, despite my voracious appetite for both, because that is not allowed.

You play the violin all your life, does anybody call you a violinist? Suck one cock—BRANDED, that's how the old joke goes, and I love old jokes and now I am one.

And if you ask me if I pity myself, I will say to you, goddamned right I do.

And if you ask me if I despise myself for the things I've done and the men and women I've slept with and hurt, inevitably, how could I not, I will tell you.

But if you ask me if I despise you, the answer is, often, yes. Sometimes I despise even the few who are left whom I hold dear in my heart. I despise them and love them at the same time. I think of every person I have loved every day, and every night I keep them in my prayers.

No woman will touch me because I may have known someone who knew someone who slept with someone who had *it,* and men will not touch me because I am somehow a betrayal of their fucking lifestyle. Because I do not like sitting around the pool at Joshua Tree with an all-male group in white linen, with identical bodies and identical patterns of speech. I stepped outside the logo-strangled tribe once too often and I am not to be trusted and now it's over, anyway. I am too old to care. Not too old to want, but too old to care. People think that, as you age, the fire of your passions burns down to ash in the grate, but it is not true. It rather quickens and intensifies, like a pasta sauce you have let reduce on the stove to bring out its richest, fullest flavors.

And, after all the funerals, and after 700,000 deaths, starting with those forty-three in 1981, starting with Patient Zero, starting twenty years before that in Africa, still fifty thousand people get it every year in this country, this country where we never even think about it anymore, and all of Africa is dying and who cares, and we go to our jobs and lie in our beds at night and remember one night, one late night at Studio in the balcony with my friend Nancy on one side and some bartender on the other and how can you help but not miss it.

I was there.

I remember.

Who the fuck wouldn't remember. Nobody does, now, these laughing, ageless boys with their sleek haircuts and their jobs in advertising and their weddings in the *Times*, but how could they? Forget? How could they affront their fathers, their brothers, the men who fucking invented them?

We look through the paper-thin slices of lime you hold in your beautiful teeth and we spit on you. Because you know nothing. Because you forgot. You didn't know?

The men who survived, only to find their relationships and desires a burning crude-oil wasteland around them— forever? The men who never got their mojo back, who wake up now in a cold sweat of remorse, survivor's guilt? Men who cannot look another man in the eye without seeing the shadow of the virus floating there? These people were, are still in some cases, *friends* of mine, and we are, even to each other, aliens. For so much of what we know there are no words, not one gesture to hold the heart together. Not anymore.

Matthew, are you there? Will you ever be home? I think about this all the time. Rick? Who got the Mercedes? Billy, have you seen Tony? Has anybody seen Billy? He doesn't answer. And Morgan, where in France are you and will you be gone long? Gone forever? Who will cut my hair?

And I knew, when I first read the article in 1981, July 3rd, the day before Independence day, about the poor forty-three who had been diagnosed with a mysterious "gay cancer," that I had the disease in me, that I had carried it since I was a child, lying dormant, and that every woman and every man that I had slept with was going to die, just as I was going to die.

I not only had the plague, ran my thinking, I *was* the plague. I had pawned my moral compass for a pair of shoes and a gold Rolex, and the devil had me by the balls, brass though they may be.

But I didn't die. My lovers didn't die. I, in fact, thrived.

My years of apprenticeship were over, and as people died all around me, as we crossed the street when we passed St. Vincent's Hospital, the money just started to pour in. Like a septic system that gets stopped up, the shit was everywhere, covering everything with green. Nobody ever mentions it, but there is no color more beautiful.

It was the year the match struck, and the flame burned brighter and hotter than it ever had before or ever would again. The Firm was inventing, every day, new instruments, as they called them, for duping and doping the rich, betting against their own bets, knowing that the house never loses. To be a client of The Firm, to allow them to move your money from square to square on the invisible chess board with lightning speed, with the speed of a con artist hiding a pea under a thimble, you had to have $20 million in your account at all times. That's a lot of toys to play with. And nobody played harder than me. I could guarantee investors 10 or 12 percent on their capital, knowing that The Firm could make at least twice that, just from keeping the money moving at lightning speed, and that a frightening chunk of that change would find its way into my pocket by the end of the year, on the day the bonuses were handed out. A yard, two yards. A fucking touchdown.

This is the way we live now. It is how our lives tick. Once there was freedom of desire, a sweetness in the skin. These are gone. Gone also is the invitation to the dance; the music has stopped. Gone also is the blue sky, the crystal water. Gone is Harbour Island, and Pink Sands, where the serving woman asked, in your cottage in the palm grove, what you would like for breakfast as she left for the night with a wave. Gone is Max's Kansas City, and sitting in the back room with Anna and Sharon, gin and tonics and cocaine and tarot. Things diffuse, some nights we just can't hold on anymore, grip any harder, fight any more savagely.

Every minor cut is watched to see if it will heal. Every cough is a death rattle.

Gone is the beauty and insatiability of fucking a stranger. Nights with women. Nights with men. The heartbeat of a decade dead in your chest. Now every touch, each kiss, is fused with a disaster that whispers in your ear and pulls you out of the sea of flesh. It is the death of pleasure, and there is not one person who is not infected.

Suddenly, everybody is carrying condoms, something you haven't done since high school, and sex is only the prelude to the dread you know you are going to feel.

You should call your doctor, schedule a test. You do nothing. In these early days, the test takes a week for the results to come back, a week during which there is no other thought in your brain except the virus floating in your blood on a slide under a microscope.

First your hair cutter dies, Benjamin Moss, a scrappy little English guy, and that's a bummer, because he cut your hair just right, and also because, in New York, changing your hairdresser is harder than changing your religion. And then everybody else dies. They die and then they stay dead.

Gone is your heart, the hopes of your youth. You tell yourself you are not a homosexual. This is not happening to you. And then Shirts, your favorite bartender, husband to three, father to seven, dies after having pneumonia eight times in six months, and you go to your first memorial in St. Patrick's Cathedral, with bagpipers playing "Amazing Grace," all of it paid for by his friends, ten thousand dollars is the rumor, as seven tough Irish American children sob uncontrollably at the loss of their father, and you think well, maybe. Maybe that one time. Maybe that other time. Who can remember all the times?

Outside, on the steps of the church, Steven says, "Who knew Shirts was a queer?" and you wonder whether any of the seven children he fathered carries the disease.

The papers say the virus can live in a teardrop. A sneeze,

and you know you should be tested but you don't go. You have wept, and sneezed, and exchanged bodily fluids with perfect strangers, men and women, and there is a cold spike in your heart that you do not pull out.

Suddenly, love is fatal. How are we to live? You work out harder at the gym. You avoid crowds. Something is broken in you and it will never be made whole again. You have the rest of your life to live, years and years, and they stretch out in front of you, barren.

Then my friend Adrienne gets it, one night with the wrong man she swears, and she dies over and over, only to be dragged back to the living every time. She is spared the blisters and blossoms of Kaposi's sarcoma, but here she is, twenty-five and she is both dying and a hypochondriac, and our blithe friendship is strained.

It's two in the morning. The phone by the bed in the Hovel rings.

"My veins are too blue."

"Adrienne, it's two o'clock in the morning. I'm sure you're fine."

"I've been watching them for two hours and they just keep getting bigger and bluer. Can you come over? I'm scared." This from a spoiled, aggressive girl who isn't afraid to make the same hairdresser "fix" her hair color four and five times in a week.

"You've been looking at your veins for how long?"

"Two hours."

"Where are you, exactly, in your apartment?"

"The bathroom."

"What kind of light is in the bathroom?"

"I don't know. Fluorescent. I guess."

"Do me a favor. Walk into your sitting room and look at them under a normal light."

A pause while Adrienne scoops up the tiny dog that never leaves her side and moves to her other phone in the sitting room. The click of a lamp and then, "Oh. Oh. They look fine."

"It was the light, Adrienne. The fluorescent light. Now go to sleep."

"Thank you for being there."

"Good night. Angels on your pillow."

And then Adrienne is in the intensive care unit at St. Vincent's, tiny, no bigger than a pencil, and I am alone and Carmela is irrevocably gone, and I don't know what to do. Not about anything.

I look at my own veins. They're blue. They carry the blood to my heart. I have no heart. Not anymore. I have no job and no future. I am thirty-six years old and I have a $300,000 car and a wardrobe that would fill a museum and I haven't the faintest idea of what to do, become, be, love.

The days are racing by, and with every day, more money gone. In New York, if you're not working, you're spending. I imagine the moment there is nothing. Terror. I get drunk in the morning and stay drunk, driving my car through the jammed streets of a hostile city, miraculously unscathed. There is a certain excitement at the thought of the vast nothingness the future holds.

I have dinner with friends, paying for everybody over their weak protests. I want disaster. I want death, a finiteness to this agony.

And, every day, more die, die hideous deaths, more often than not alone. It started with a look, a tightness of the skin across the cheekbones, and suddenly the virus was visible, and then we all had the look, and there was no touch that was not suspect, no gesture that did not cause suspicion.

Kurt Cobain sang, "Everybody's gay," *In Utero*, 1993, but by that time it was too late, and we could only hear, "Everybody's dying."

Nobody remembers it now. An entire generation of men walking in a wasteland. The young men now, they are so smug, so self-satisfied. Their skin will never be covered with running sores. They have unsafe sex, playing the odds, knowing that the result, even if they get the virus, is no more than a chronic condition, like diabetes.

Adrienne lay in her bed at St. Vincent's, hooked up to

an array of tubes, and I sent her a flat of tulips to cheer her up. She didn't like the color. She ripped out her IV tube, screaming. She sent them back. Demanded new ones, and of course she got them.

These are not my people, I told myself again and again, memory selecting what to keep and what to discard.

But, in the dark, in the dead of night in my narrow bed in the apartment I said I would never live in again, I hear their voices. I hear them talk to me. They say: they die, and then they stay dead.

Wish me luck, the same to you.

CHAPTER EIGHTEEN

Table Hopping

❖　❖　❖

I t started very badly and it went on for a very long
time. The end was kind of fun, in a career-wrecker
kind of way, but traveling the distance from two hostile men sitting at a conference table over espresso to the
throwing up in the street part just took fucking forever.

First of all, my Hermès scarf tie was just all wrong. Dick
Morris, my client, had made his fortune by owning the most
Laundromats of anybody in the world, he lived in Beanstalk,
Idaho, or somewhere, and was a wildly alcoholic man of
simple tastes. The scarf tie was a show of ostentation that
was bound to raise his hackles, even if he didn't exactly
know its provenance. It just looked too expensive, and, in

Dick's eyes, had been bought with his money, a useless, foppish waste by a city slicker, the man who was supposed to be making his money grow to even more gargantuan size. Then there was the Brioni suit I wore, the shoes polished to a lacquered gloss, wrong, all of it, all wrong. Dick Morris, with his shapeless hopsack suit and his Florsheim shoes, found my attire inappropriate for a heart-to-heart chat, even if he had flown to New York on his own jet, landing at Teterboro in a fog, both meteorological and alcoholic.

We sat in a conference room high up into that fog, and went through his handsomely extended portfolio line by line. At about line 200, Dick Morris put down his retractable pencil and said, "Scotch." A glass of eighteen-year-old on a silver tray was put in front of him by a white-coated waiter. "Fuck the ice and leave the bottle" was all he said. It was ten thirty in the morning.

I was dying for a drink, even though I was still a tad tipsy from the night before, which had ended about five. I could feel the sweat pool at my sacroiliac, my carefully fitted shirt wilting, even in the chill of the conference room. Dick Morris was a strong, rich man, affable enough, fun, even, at times. His theory was: How can you stay drunk all day unless you start drinking in the morning?

The conference lasted seven hours, during which he consumed the entire bottle of Scotch. We got to the end and began a discussion of the tax implications of the buying and selling and rearranging we had been doing for the past lifetime, me sober as a Wheatie, Dick drunker and more irascible by the hour. I tried to explain them, but he cut me short.

He spoke with the overly accurate diction of a man who has been drinking for seven hours. "Taxation is robbery. How much are they going to rob me of this year?"

"It's the price we pay for living in a free society," I said.

"I will go to my grave without ever giving a penny to those goddamned people in Washington. I don't believe in government. Blood-sucking bastards, every one of them. I haven't voted in twenty years. Are you a child? Make it go away, or I'm taking my marbles across the street. I give you a gift, a fucking bull's-eye, and you expect me to pay taxes? *Taxes?* Taxes are for fools."

He drained his glass for maybe the three-dozenth time.

"So where are we eating? I hate the food in New York. I hate New York."

I suggested several places. Places it was impossible to get into, unless you knew the number that was the real number, not the one in the phone book, the line that never got answered.

"We're going, son, to the Russian Tea Room. Now *that's* a restaurant."

It was five o'clock. My stomach churned at the thought of food, but brightened at the sound of a single word—cocktails. Dick Morris was one of those clients you didn't have to worry about getting drunk around; he would do nothing more than welcome the company. He drank with a thirst that was gargantuan.

The car dropped us at five forty-five. And we entered the restaurant's giant room, all red, hung year-round with Christmas decorations. Tinsel swagged from every beam, crimson-faced waiters in scarlet hussar uniforms circled the room. When it came to venomous service and inflated prices, nothing beat the RTR, and I began to settle into that feeling of being in exactly the right place at the right time.

An icy bottle of vodka was brought to the table, and caviar was heaped on plates with ice cream scoops. Dick ate and drank ravenously, the prices meaning nothing. He figured with $350 mil stashed at The Firm, it was only our duty to show him a good time, and, if the Russian Tea Room had offered lap dancers, he would have had several along with his caviar. That not being in the offing, Dick tucked in and settled down to a long evening of gastronomic pleasure with the awful food on the awful menu. The food was so bad it was kind of endearing. I was just glad to feel the first hit of vodka flooding my veins, making my heart sing.

Dick was a funny guy, meaning he could, given enough

liquor and sensual pleasure, actually be funny and likable in a polyester kind of way. Stories about his fat wife, Mamie, about his car collection, thirty-seven, and his moronic children were truly amusing, and I was suddenly glad to be in his company. A joie de vivre imbued the air, settled my stomach, and erased the day's every number from my mind. He had the air of a man who was going to finish the evening asking for a really expensive hooker, with the certain knowledge that she would be provided for him. Anything he liked would be provided for him, the Laundromat king who maybe hadn't had sex for six or eight weeks, certainly not with a smooth-skinned twenty-something girl in six-inch heels.

Borscht was served, the one thing the RTR did well, and if they had had a board announcing, like McDonald's, the number of portions served, the total would be impressive. Over a trillion sold, toyed with, and sent back to the kitchen largely untouched.

Dick asked me to order a bottle of wine, and I did, at $400. It was brought to the table with great ceremony, and uncorked, and Dick was given a taste. He swirled it in his balloon glass. He sniffed, drank, then spat it on the floor. Let me say that again. He spat it on the floor, splattering the sommelier's dusty shoes, and said, "This swill? I wouldn't drink this swill on a bet. Give this bottle to my friend here, and bring me a *real* Bordeaux. Bring me your most expensive bottle of red wine right *now*."

Tiny Armenian teenagers frantically began to scrub the ancient carpeting as the egregiously expensive bottle of wine, decades old, dusty from waiting, was brought to the table, tasted, and met with glum approval by the laundry king. "I serve better wine *at lunch*," he bellowed. *"To people I don't like."*

Suddenly: "What's your name? I'm calling you Louis."

"It's Dimitri, sir."

Dick peeled a $100 bill off of a big roll in his pocket and gave it to Dmitri. "Well, Louis, life is just too short to drink bad wine. If I wanted bad wine, I'd get poor like you."

"Yes, sir."

He tasted the wine that was poured. "Drinkable. Not great, but drinkable. Now get these damned kids away from me and bring some food."

He sent everything back at least once. The vodka had kicked in, and I began to like Dick and his $350 mil a lot. Underneath his baggy suit, he was a good guy. Fun-loving. Vulgar. Dumb as a dryer. And, with him drinking like a fish, he wouldn't notice how much I was knocking back or how many times I went to the bathroom to freshen up.

There was something uber-bizarre about being in the old Russian Tea Room. All those Christmas decorations. All those octogenarian waiters, all called Dimitri or Boris. Lost in time. Lost in an alcoholic haze that made forty bucks for a bowl of soup seem reasonable. Those were the days when expense accounts were endless, nobody really paid for anything, except some poor guy in Denver who was watching Monday-night football, unaware that $400 bottles of wine were being spit on the floor, staining the thousand-year-old raggedy carpeting. We had blini with the golfball caviar, several times, and we had borscht and we had shashlik and strogonoff, and a lot of other stuff I didn't even know the name of. Waiters swirled around the table like bees at honey time, placing and replacing the enormous, heavy restaurant silver.

Dick told me how his wife Mamie was in bed—not so hot—and how he was in bed when he was with women other than Mamie—fantastic—and how big his dick was—enormous, much bigger than mine and this I know for a fact because we went to the bathroom and compared. He was a stubby little man with a lot of washers and dryers and a big dick, and all of this was making Dick happier and happier as the night wore on, although my mood darkened when I realized, in the size department, both of portfolio and of member, I would never be where Dick was, that is, on top of the fucking world.

Even the Dimitris and Boris's started to like Dick, the

more times he reached into his pocket and peeled off more bills. He would do it at odd moments, did it as though in passing, "Here, Louie," he would say, to some sadsack waiter who just happened to be passing by. "Go wild. Bring me another bottle of that wine." When all that was gone, he asked for some even more obscure, ridiculous vintage and of course they had it.

The Christmas lights began to sparkle and whirl, and I could tell the moment was approaching when Dick stopped sending his food back and began to make subtle and then not so subtle hints about Russian girls and all that he had heard about their beauty and licentiousness.

"You have to taste this fish," he said.

I declined, twice, but he insisted, and then he picked up a big gob of some sort of fish in a heavy cream sauce in his fork and deposited it on the tablecloth. "Eat that," he said. "It's heaven." And, once scraped off the tablecloth, it kind of was.

Dick and I were having fun. At least it seemed so at the time. The other patrons of the restaurant found it not so much fun, and began to call for their checks.

A girl was mentioned by one of the Louies, and then a girl was found, she'd be here in half an hour, nineteen, and capable of tricks and pleasures unseen in any non-Asiatic country, anywhere. She would be in this very room in forty-five minutes. And, stomach churning from all the caviar and the steaming dishes that weren't hot enough or too salty, and the expensive wine I had personally packed away, along with two grams of Peru's finest Marching Powder, I decided that what the evening needed, to pass the time from brandy to Natasha, was some entertainment provided by me personally. So I jumped on the red banquette and hopped on the table and sang, at the top of my voice, "Hava Nagila," which, thanks to thousands of duty bar and bat mitzvahs I had attended, I actually knew the words to, at least the "Hava Nagila" part. The room, almost empty, really cleared out fast, so we were the only customers left.

The disaster that wrecks you can be a big thing, or a small thing. Sometimes, it's hardly even remarked upon. The thread snaps, and the button falls to the ground. You don't even notice. The blister that's been bothering you for weeks suddenly pops. Sometimes you say the unsayable, the thing that, once said, cannot be unsaid. You say it not because it's clever or apt or kind. You say it simply because it's there, hanging in the air, waiting to be said. You drop the bomb. You fuck up at work and can't find anybody else to blame it on. Me, I danced.

In what even I, through the fog, knew to be a misguided adventure, I danced. I got up on the banquette, tearing the hundred-year-old leather, where every famous behind in New York had sat, at some time, along with thousands of wide-eyed tourists, and then I clambered onto the small round table, and I danced the Kazatsky, booming "Hava Nagila" in the full-throated cry of my youth and enthusiasm. How else could I express my joy at having spent the evening with Dick Morris, laundry king, and soon-to-be-laid Midwestern schlub extraordinaire. At that moment, I loved Dick Morris.

Stemware and crockery flew everywhere, smashing into a thousand bits and sending the Algerian boys into fits of overtime. There was general alarm in the restaurant, alarm that in no way weakened my enthusiasm for my melodious exertions. I was, at 185 pounds of solid-packed muscle, a challenge for the small round table, which suddenly gave way, landing me on my backside amidst the carnage, cutting a wide gash in my suit, not to mention my ass. My butt would need stitches; the boxers were beyond repair, a heartbreak, my favorite pair.

Just as the table collapsed, Natasha arrived, a stunning girl with a wildly unnatural mane of blonde hair, wearing a micro-leather skirt, pink, with a purple chubby fur jacket and more eye makeup than is normally in stock at Bloomingdale's. Dick Morris laughed uproariously, sobering up slightly at the sight of Natasha and her bodyguard, who was introduced as her uncle. The kind of burly man who could

squash a Volkswagen with one hand, a man with hair grow-
ing out of both his ears and his nostrils, sprouting as well
out of the sagging neckline of his heavy sweater. There may
have been a gun in there. I'm pretty sure there was.

It took two hussars and two Armenians to get me off
the floor, still attempting the Kazatsky even in the ruination
of blood and glassware. I had no wish to stop dancing, even
as it became obvious that all Dick wanted was to get to the
Marriott Times Square where he, ever thrifty, stayed, and
be alone with the luscious Natasha. I waved my American
Express card at them, and they brightened considerably and
returned instantaneously. Everything was hilarious, but the
figure at the bottom of the bill was especially hilarious, four
thousand in wine alone, over five total for a quiet, barely ed-
ible and largely untouched dinner for two. I tipped in cash,
as Ford Madox Ford advised.

Uncle Hairy accepted the huge wad of bills Dick put in
his hand, without counting it; even he had some politesse.
Natasha spoke no English, but made it clear that she was
ready to shed her chubby and get down to business with
Dick, over whom she towered.

It took an army to get us out the door, even after they
saw the fabulous pile of cash I had left as expiation. I somehow had a strand of tinsel around my neck, and blood gush-
ing from my rear end.

On the street outside, the car still waited. The dinner

had gone on for six hours, and the driver was asleep, but, once wakened, he could see he had a situation on his hands. "Great night," said Dick, just as I threw up on his shoes.

"Fuck, man," he said. "That was truly uncalled for." He took off his shoes and socks and, in a Herculean display of athleticism, threw them into the middle of Fifty-Seventh Street. "Not acceptable," he said, as he got into the stretch barefoot with Natasha and crept off into the night, leaving me bleeding and broken on the curb. I waved a feeble good-bye, and something told me it really was good-bye.

The emergency room removed the shards of glass from my behind, asking no explanation with none given, and sent me home with seven stitches at three in the morning. A long haul for a night of revelry that had started early that morning. It seemed, now, so far in the distant past.

The sheets were silken and cool, Carmela slept peacefully, her hair, her skin, radiant in the glow of the streetlights, more beautiful than a thousand Natashas. Moonlight. Milk. The petals of white peonies. A woman of qualities. I imagined her in a short purple fur, and I wanted desperately to bathe my wounds in the sweetness of her waters, and tried to wake her, but she shrugged me off.

"You're drunk," she said. "I was drunk but now I'm asleep. Leave a girl alone for once." I tried to sleep, but there was no way, so at six thirty I got up and gingerly showered and appeared at work at seven thirty, except there was no way I could sit in an office chair, and one guy stopped by, took one look, and said, observing the various cuts, abrasions, and bruises on my face, "I want to see the other guy," so I hadn't quite gotten away with the night of revelry.

At nine, there was a brief meeting at which I was told I had been asked off of Dick Morris's account but, not to worry, there was lots of other room to grow and ply my satanic wares. I could make a rock make money, they said. I sent Dick Morris a gift certificate for a pair of John Lobb shoes and went on, standing, with my day, wielding complex financial instruments like Obi-Wan Kenobi's sword of light.

But it was over and I knew it. If you think you're going to get fired, you are, in fact, going to get fired, and, as the days passed and I behaved myself with an absolute rigor, word began to get around and the myth grew, and within four months, slowly stripped of account after account, I was called into the office for the last time.

So quick bright things come to confusion. So quick.

CHAPTER NINETEEN

What They Sing About, When They Sing in Heaven

❖ ❖ ❖

I
t is axiomatic that, just because you lose all your
money, just because you are suddenly stripped of your
place in the world, it doesn't mean your friends lose
everything, too. No siree, Bob. They do not.

The morning after you get fired, you wake up back in
Hovel Hall, where the rats and roaches, in your absence,
have apparently done nothing but multiply and grow less
timid. You know that, by 7:45 a.m., you are already past
tense at The Firm. You have simply ceased to be, your office
bare, your friends averting their eyes when they pass your
door.

Yesterday, when you were still in the present tense, in

the land of the living, there was much collegial backslap-
ping and high-fiving and dewy-eyed hugging with your colleagues. You were still a person, a friend.

The looks began to grow more distant, the high-fiving
nonexistent as they watched you return to your office,
where the phone had already been shut off, the Rolodex
confiscated, and an armed guard stood at the portal of what
was once the seat of your power. The head of HR was there,
trying to look sympathetic, but let's face it, she, with her
$42,000-a-year life—lived principally with cats and cross-
words and Beaujolais—must get such glee out of watching
the mighty with their tails between their legs.

"I'm so sorry," she said, firm and confident, "You have
to clear out your office. They want you out by noon."

Looking around at all that stuff made you want to
throw up. "Belinda, love of my life. I'm not packing up
anything. You know what belongs to The Firm. The rest is
mine. Get some grunt to box it up and send it to me as soon
as possible." Not knowing that she would be sending the
stuff to a loft where Carmela was already having the locks
changed, having received a call from a friend and set her
course of action—possess the loft, strip the bank accounts
of cash, cut my face out of the wedding pictures, things
that women know to do. She was on the phone every five
minutes with Gloria, her mother, who'd been through it all

twice, plotting it all out, where to transfer the money so I couldn't get at it, stuff like that.

I was to get nothing, except, of course, the bills for maintaining it all. She got the lap pool at eighty degrees in January.

"Here's what we do," said Fanelli, who was one of the genuinely dewy-eyed ones. "You get four rolls of quarters and then we go to the nearest Irish bar and get shitfaced and you call every headhunter and trader you know. You got to move fast, bro'. Don't let the Wookie win."

Seven martinis and a hundred quarters later, not one headhunter or trader—people I had known for years, the same people who were calling me a week ago to entice me to switch jobs—not one of these fine people had even deigned to take my call. To them as well, I had vanished. They knew there was no higher rung on the trading ladder to be thrown off of than The Firm, and that it was impossible to climb back up. Ever. Not even if I went to the Trappist monastery in Gethsemani, Kentucky, where the Dalai Lama holes up when he's in town and where they make the fruitcakes one gets relentlessly at Christmas, not even if I took a vow of chastity and silence, not even then would I ever get another job, not on The Street.

The sun just beginning to slant, we went to Tenth Avenue and I bought the fancy car, which I couldn't afford and which lost half its value the second the tires hit the asphalt, and we rolled through the streets and bars and clubs like kings until four.

I woke up the next morning in the suit I had worn the day before, sprawled half on and half off the sofa in the Hovel. We, Fanelli and I, had traveled the length and breadth of the city in the new car, which was probably parked somewhere near to where I lay; no matter how drunk you are, you don't lose a car, at least you don't lose it forever. There were many empty bottles of fancy liquor rolling around on the floor, indicating the presence of recent company, but who they were, or when they had arrived and done whatever they did, I couldn't have told you. The apartment was in every way worse than it had ever been.

There are some apartments that, once you've moved out of them, become so radioactive you could never live there again. Hovel Hall, by dawn's light, had the greenish glow of nuclear fission.

Things you learn when you're unemployed: a watched pot *will* boil. It just takes a very, very long time, time being what you have a lot of. Second thing: a million dollars isn't really very much money. Third thing: work may be heinous, but it gives you someplace to go in the morning, a reason to get up and shave and leave the apartment, not to mention that they pay you.

These thoughts brought on the plan for revenge. I would show them, or so I thought. Get a better job. Have harder abs. Rent a house on the beach in East Hampton and allow them to come and sponge off me. I was so young, hardly begun. I was very, very good at the thing I did. It was unthinkable that life as I knew it was over. This was only a minor interruption on the road. A speed bump.

After four days of self-pity and rats, I did the only sensible thing: I moved into the Pierre Hotel, a Four Seasons property at the time. Staggering flower arrangements. Staggering room rates. Staggeringly obsequious service. God bless the Platinum Card from American Express.

I rented a suite, a big one, overlooking the zoo in Central Park. From the bathroom, you could see all the way to Harlem, and at night, the glow of the city lights lulled me to sleep as though in a mother's arms, imagining all the festive parties the gang was going to have in my little slice of heaven on the 37th floor. A foyer, a big sitting room furnished with that kind of furniture so popular in English country houses, the same art on every wall in every room.

It was going to be great. Elegant. People would come over and cavort until the small hours. Champagne Brut in the minifridge, long lines of cocaine on the glass-topped cocktail table. Super Bowl parties. Like a clubhouse with room service. The staid pictures on the cream-colored walls would look down nightly on scenes of such debauchery they would blush with shame and turn their faces to the wall.

I kept $2,000 in cash in my pocket at all times. There's no money like cash money, Shirts used to say. The other thing he used to advise was that one should never tip a bartender with coins. Coins were trash, to be swept onto the floor for the busboys to clean up.

The $100 bills in my pocket were like condoms for my self-esteem. The smaller bills were there for the endless tipping involved in living in the Pierre Hotel. It cost me, on average, about sixty bucks to get from my room to the street, more if it was raining and I wanted a cab. This made the staff unbelievably deferential to me, greeting me respectfully by name every time they saw me.

The hotel even moved a baby grand piano into the vast sitting room of the suite, so that Fanelli could sing when he wanted to, which was any time anybody asked him. He adored Anthea, but she wouldn't let him smoke in their apartment, so he bought a dog, and every night he'd walk the dog down to the Pierre and join in the fun, smoking a fat cigar while the doorman watched the dog. Every night was a fiesta, music by Fanelli. He couldn't really have thought he was fooling his wife, but I guess, even early on, there are secret arrangements that are made between married people.

Just stepping out of the revolving door of the hotel was

a thrill, after a dozen sharply worded good-mornings. Out-side was Madison Avenue, the street of dreams. I would wander Madison Avenue every day, drooling at the collec-tion of shops and the merchandise therein. I would pre-tend I had ten thousand dollars, and see how many blocks it would take before the imaginary ten thousand was spent. Some days, I could get all the way to Ninety-Sixth street. Some days I couldn't even go a block. I bought myself a present every day.

I sent out a hundred résumés, accompanied by a fine letter with the Pierre's logo embossed on the eager cover letter. Then I waited. And still I waited. Nothing came back, not a word. I gave out the Pierre's number, thinking it added a touch of gloss. Nothing. Sometimes I would take a nap in the afternoon, and ask the telephone operator to hold any calls until I let her know. It was a useless thing to do. There was never a call.

Still, it was going to be great. They even let me smoke in the room, which was a thing that was increasingly hard to come by. Smoking was being stamped out everywhere, one of life's great pleasures, but in really expensive hotels they still let you smoke. I delighted in every puff. I was rid-ing a river of cash that was without end, or so I told myself, except in the dead of night when the cold sweats came and I calculated exactly how far I was from zero.

Security at the hotel was almost invisible, making you think you roamed free and safe in a blessed and fragrant meadow, filled with those enormous flower arrangements, although there must have been a thousand eyes following your every move. So you had to be careful who you brought home with you, you didn't want to sully the splendor and grace of the hallways with the wrong kind of riffraff. I brought somebody home every night, women, men, sometimes both. Fantastic men and women you paid money to have sex with, paid in cash and cocaine. The staff and the elevator operators never said a word. At Christmas, I gave everybody who could walk fifty dollars, and I gave Mr. Papandreou, the manager of the hotel, five hundred. I put a tree in the room, and we all decorated it, and the hotel sent champagne and a cake. It was like being Eloise with six-pack abs.

It was the perfect way to live. I might as well have taken all my money and put it in the middle of Fifth Avenue and poured gasoline on it and set it on fire. I woke up every morning terrified that this time I had caught AIDS from a hooker, but I still brought them home with me almost every night. I didn't want to sleep alone. I was lonely. And there was such marvelous beauty to be had.

Then, one night in January—it was snowing, I remember—I met Casey on Lexington Avenue, strolling and trolling with the other hookers. The other women were warm and enticing, dark and lissome and eager. They emanated warmth and comfort.

Casey was chilly. Not little-matchstick-girl cold in any pathetic way, she just looked chilly as the snowflakes swirled around her boyishly short blonde hair, and settled, leaving diamonds of water all over her head, a sparkling tiara under the streetlight.

I stopped and said hello, in that way you do, letting her know that she was, for the night at least, the chosen one. She pulled her coat more tightly around her and said hello so softly a passing taxi whisked it away.

Something happened. I took her hand. That is never done, not ever, but she put her small, cold hand in mine as naturally as anything, and we began to walk back up Lexington and toward the hotel. We looked like any affectionate couple anywhere in the world.

I told her my name. My real name.

"Casey" was all she said.

"Well, Casey, here we are."

"And here we go."

"Again you mean."

"No. No. I didn't mean anything. Just trying to be friendly." She paused. "You say hello a lot in this business."

"Hello."

"Hello. But nobody takes your hand. Not ever."

"It's a pretty hand. Warm?"

"Warmer now. Thanks for asking. Where are we going?"

I told her and she tried not to be impressed, but you could tell she was. And you felt a loosening, a relaxing of her guard. Nothing bad would happen to her at the Pierre. Nothing bad ever happened to anybody at the Pierre.

We walked along in the snow. "It's nice, though," she said.

"What?"

"Holding hands. Nobody wants to touch you except when, you know, when they're fucking you."

"You looked cold."

"Most people wouldn't notice. To them you're only one thing. A catalog of body parts."

We got to the hotel, and went to my room. Casey admired the view, and looking down at all the rooftop gardens, winter now, she said that one day she was going to have a garden like that. Casey looked at the Fifty-Ninth Street Bridge, hazy in the snow and the mist, and mentioned Georgia O'Keeffe.

Then we took our clothes off. She liked a dim room, and I did, too, that moment when the shadows disappear into dark and you're living solely in the land of touch and desire.

She was terrible in bed. Not for lack of trying, or even pliability and kindness, but this was a girl who wasn't going to win any awards at the Hooker Ball.

She tried. Her body drew warmth from mine and her skin became like a dawn rose. But she knew none of the tricks of the trade, the oh baby's and special posturing and entreaties that made most good hookers worth the five hundred dollars. She didn't know, as they did, how to make you feel, in that moment, in that slanting light and swirl of snow, to make you feel like the only man on earth.

Casey was an amateur, and that kind of turned me on, but the more I approached, the more my body sang, the deafer she became.

I drew away. "I know," she said. "I'm not very good, am I? Most men don't care. They just don't tip me. I don't do this because I want to. It's OK. You don't have to pay me. It's not your fault. You are . . ." she thought for a minute, ". . . *éblouissant.*"

"What's that?"

"It's French. Means 'dazzling.'"

She got out of bed and began to collect her things. In the dim light, her body was lovely, ghostlike, sturdy but not thick, the body of an Eakins schoolboy, except for the breasts, which were firm and full, and hung from her chest with the kind of loft that vanishes before twenty-five.

"Why do you do it?"

Her clothes were bunched in front of her breasts, making me want to see them again, wishing the scenario had played out in other ways. Still, I'd spent five hundred dollars on more stupid things than Casey, and I didn't feel cheated. There is such an abundance of loveliness in the world. Too much, actually.

"To pay for my lessons. Singing lessons."

"You sing?"

"*Oui.*" Jean Seberg, that was it. Jean Seberg in *Breathless*.

"Sing for me."

"I will, if that's what you want. It's my best thing. Maybe you won't feel so . . . so disappointed."

"Trust me. I have plenty of sex. I'm not disappointed. Not at all."

We moved to the sitting room. In the darkened room, the sky from the thirty-seventh floor glowed with an interminable and ineffable beauty. The moving flakes. So many lives so far below us. People hurrying. People fucking or fighting in the next room.

She sat at the piano. Naked, she felt the keys, she moved her fingers gently in the air as though trying to catch a moth without causing it harm.

Playing softly, she sang. "When this old world gets tired and mean . . ." She sang "Up on the Roof" and, had he been there, Fanelli would have thought he'd died and gone to heaven.

They say Nina Simone had it. Callas. Marvin Gaye and James Taylor. Mandy Patinkin. They have something in their voices that is beyond music, that transcends notes and cadence and melody and has the power to kill you and bring you back to life all in the same breath.

Maybe it was an illusion, maybe she was just a pretty girl with an average voice in the night. Maybe it was the warm, naked flesh and the swirling snow and the lives and dreams of all the people of New York in 1987 who were not here at this moment. Maybe it wasn't her voice, which was undeniably beautiful. It was the whole secret history of her life and what had brought her from there to here. Or it was the fact that she was producing this magic just for me, a man looking surely at the end of the rope, but I wept to hear it. All I had wanted was a quick fuck from a talented hooker. I hadn't thought. I hadn't thought that this could happen. This transient beauty, these tears in the snowstorm. I don't cry. I hadn't cried since I got fired, not when I left The Firm, not when Carmela took everything. Casey looked up, saw the tears and heard the sobs, but she said nothing. She somehow knew that I was crying for myself, not for her, and that it was a private thing, too deep and dark to touch.

She finished and began to dress. "Well," she said. "That's me, then."

This really happened, too. It happened to *me*. It's mine, and you cannot take it away from me. It was the apex of my youth. You think it's some cheesy scene out of a movie? Well, fuck you. A boyish young girl sat naked in room 3710 of the Pierre Hotel on a night in February in 1987 and sang just to me, and, when I am dying, it is this scene that I will remember with the most gratitude.

As Casey dressed, I got out my checkbook and wrote her a check for $25,000. I gave it to her as she left, made out to cash. I didn't even know her last name. I gave her my gloves, too, from Bottega Veneta, miles too big for her, and told her to stay warm. As she left, I asked her if she could come back the next night and she agreed.

We met every night, and every night the scene played out in exactly the same way. She would play and sing, and I would cry.

And she would never say a word to comfort me; her voice was all the comfort she had to give. Life existed in intervals for me: between the time I was with her and the time I wasn't. We never made another attempt at sex.

I gave a party and she came. She came and sang and enchanted a roomful of heartless, mercenary traders and their girls. They were enchanted with her, of course, every single one of them fell in love with her during that party, but with whatever shred of decency they had left, they never came on to her, assuming she was my girlfriend. Which, in a way, she was.

So for a while it was actually great. Drunken nights watching the hoops. Liquored-up orgies with women we met in bars. I paid my way, and took my pleasure in the same way I always had, but the night sweats got colder and more frequent. I realized one day that I was going to lose everything I hadn't already lost, and I sold the car, getting exactly half what I had paid for it a month before. The car had 746 miles on it.

But, whatever else, I would race home like a junkie to meet with Casey and sit naked and have her sing for me alone. Then Turner, a trader who had been on the floor about six seconds, realizing that our relationship was chaste, stepped into the scene and snatched her away from me. In time, he married her. Then I sat alone at night weeping, and the piano stood silent until I asked them to take it away.

It's a strange feeling watching the bride walking down the aisle and knowing that you've fucked her.

She ended up living in a four-bedroom penthouse on Park Avenue, wearing a heart-shaped diamond ring bigger than Dolly Parton's. She and Turner are now the other people, the people I see going into their boxes at the opera, glittering, as I walk up the stairs to the family circle, where the cheap seats are. We aren't friends, and they don't even notice me in my ordinary pants and windbreaker.

No, there is no acknowledgment. She came to me for the last time on the night before her wedding, after the rehearsal dinner, which was held in the hotel. She came and sang for me one last time, but we both sat, clothed and awkward, and her voice, pretty enough, didn't have any power over my heart anymore and my crying days were over.

Two years later, she somehow found me again, and sent me a check for $25,000 along with a recording of her voice singing "Up on the Roof." There was no note.

I maxed out my credit cards. I applied for others, more and more obscure ones, and maxed them out one by one.

Then the phone calls started coming. I had thought I was protected, but evil Carmela gave out my whereabouts, and, every morning, I had to deal with a lot of harsh criticism from men and women in places like Cleveland, who wanted me to give them money.

Then the mother of them all, American Express, turned off the faucet on my platinum card. I owed them $56,000, of which I had three thousand in the bank and the thousand in my pocket.

There were acres of beautiful things, like Charvet shirts and Armani suits I had never even worn, hanging in the overflowing closets, and I realized with regret that clothing was not real estate. It was not a negotiable or fungible item.

Within minutes of the call from Mrs. American Express, there was a knock on the door, and I opened it to find an extremely nervous Mr. Papandreou.

"Sir, most regrettable, this visit. It's about your bill."

"I know. I just got a call from American Express."

"Do you have another credit card we might use?"

"I'm afraid not."

"Any other form of compensation?"

"None."

"We've enjoyed your company, but . . ."

"I know. When?"

"By three o'clock. That's all we can allow for late checkout."

"Today?"

"Unless you have some other way to pay."

"I'll need some help. There's a lot of stuff."

"Whatever you need, don't hesitate to ask. You have been a special friend to the Pierre."

Within minutes a housemaid and two bellmen were in the suite, helping me to pack. When we were done, I gave each of them fifty dollars and by two fifteen I was on the street with six suitcases and four hanging bags, getting into the complimentary shuttle that the hotel offered to its special guests. Every staff member shook my hand as I passed through the lobby, some even hugged and kissed me. One asked if I needed any money. My face colored with shame and embarrassment. But I took the fifty he offered.

Given midtown traffic, it took a while to get home. Isaac, the driver, who had carried me to clubs nobody had even heard the name of yet, would not shut up the whole way about how better days were just around the corner.

I knew better. If you let life do to you whatever it wants, it can do some terrible things.

Hovel Hall was one of those terrible things that life can do to you: 53 West Thirty-Fifth Street, fifth floor. When I was really drunk, it was impossible to enunciate even my own address.

Isaac offered to help with the luggage, but he had a bad back and wore a brace and I couldn't do that, so I gave him fifty, and waved good-bye as though I were setting sail for Europe on the *Île de France*. As I was carrying the first two suitcases up the five flights of stairs to the apartment, crackheads stole all the rest. Good-bye, Brioni. Good-bye, Charvet. Good-bye, Armani and all the rest, a fortune's worth of clothes.

My grandfather's gold watch was in one of those suitcases. It meant the world to me, that watch.

Hello, Honey! Hello, I'm home.

CHAPTER TWENTY

The Eleven-Foot Hooker
Walks the Walk

❖   ❖   ❖

T he street was not a solid thing. It was fluid as a river, an undulation of asphalt and cement, swarming with rats and crackheads and hookers. You could feel the waves in your body. Nothing was stable or solid, all was moving, hawking, fighting, stealing. The first year back in the Hovel, I was mugged five times on my own block. Twice in broad daylight, once with a knife at my throat. I learned to carry enough cash on me that the average crackhead would be satisfied with his take, but not so much money that my thin bank account would be drained in a single snatch, a late-night grab.

One mugging, in broad daylight, was so cleverly done I

was stupefied. A man bumped into me, nudged my shoulder. Not an unusual thing on a busy street. At that exact instant, two other guys grabbed my arms, one apiece and pulled them behind me, while a fourth shot his hands in my pockets and pulled out the cash that was there. Over in ten seconds. Brilliant.

Now that credit cards are everything and nobody ever carries cash anymore, the mugging profession must be in decline.

There were two hotels on the street where I lived, and four parking garages, so the din was unbearable at any hour. In the day, there was an incessant honking of horns, since, because of the parking garages, traffic crept along, often not moving a foot from light to light, and at night the monster garbage trucks roared their omnivorous way down the block at a creeping pace, stopping every ten yards to hoist mountains of garbage into their yawning, straining maws.

I read Proust and waited for the phone to ring, or a letter to come in response to my résumé. It took six months to read all of Proust, during which time not one phone call or letter came. It is my unshakeable conviction that *À La Recherche du Temps Perdu* is the greatest single work of art of the twentieth century. It is also my unshakeable conviction that all debt collectors, of whom I got to know many, were bullied in grade school.

So I read Proust and got mugged. Those were my principal activities that year. Both were deep and lasting learning experiences.

I also learned that it was safer, when walking home drunk from the bars, to walk in the middle of the street. At two in the morning, there was little traffic and, in the street, it was more of an effort to pull you into a doorway and put a knife to your throat.

Which is how I got to know the hookers.

Thirty-Fifth Street was a United Nations of hookers. Women of every ethnic and cultural and sexual variety walked the streets, usually down the center, scattering when a car raced past, then returning to their languid stroll on the asphalt. They carried tiny purses. They sucked on lollipops. There was one year when they all, strangely, sucked on baby pacifiers. They would yell at the passing cars, show lewd body parts, make irresistible offers to taillights racing home to New Jersey.

Some cars crept down the street, on the prowl, and the hookers would walk alongside the creeping cars making deals with the skill of a Wall Street trader selling junk bonds, and, often, the car would stop and the girl would get in, twitching her behind in victory for the other girls to see, and the car would speed off into the dark, only to deliver the hooker back to the flock half an hour later.

One girl stood head and shoulders above the rest. Literally. She must have been six four. In addition to which she wore cork platform shoes with the highest heels I've ever seen. And she was not petite. She was gargantuan. Vast. Enormous.

She was probably nineteen and still had the loveliness of a child.

I would walk past her and she would call out in a soft voice, "Don't you want to have a really good time? Let Holly show you a really, really good time." I didn't acknowledge her entreaties, although every now and then it would occur to me that, hell, yes, I actually would like to have a really good time. I would like to have a good time if I had the money to have a really, really good time.

Holly was magnificent in every way. On chilly nights, she wore a short coat of fake fur, pink, which did nothing to keep her long legs warm, and you could tell she was cold, must have been, but, in the face of this or any other vicissitude, Holly didn't show discomfort. She walked like she was strolling on a summer's night on Worth Avenue in Palm Beach, Florida. She was the tree topper on the Christmas tree of Thirty-Fifth Street hookers. When cars approached, Holly just kept on languidly strolling down the center of the street, forcing the cars to slow down, to take life at Holly's pace, until, finally, with utter insouciance, she veered slightly to the right or left to let the vehicle pass her by. Sometimes the drivers would reach out to grab her ass, but she would just swat their hands away like gnats on a summer sandwich, saying, "Oh, child," with a breathy sigh.

One night, after massive numbers of cocktails at P. J. Clark's with Fanelli, who still called, he and I stood in a drunken embrace on the street, weeping over my ill-fortune, and then we parted, him in a cab uptown, me downtown on foot since I was completely broke. When I put my hand in my jacket pocket, I felt and then pulled out five $100 bills that Fanelli had slipped in while we were weeping over the injustice of life in general and our deep and abiding affection for each other in particular. I felt like the Emperor of Ethiopia. I hadn't had that much cash on me in months. I wept at his kindness and subtlety, and hailed a taxi, an actual yellow cab. I was too drunk to say my full address, so I had him let me off on the corner of Fifth, and walked down Thirty-Fifth, the street of muggings and broken dreams, although it wasn't walking in the normal sense by any means.

Holly called out and something struck. I had five hundred dollars and I did want to have a really, really good time. I staggered toward her, and realized, up close, that Holly was a man in drag. A boy, actually. A tall boy. Well, I thought, so what.

Before I could speak, however, I fell flat on my face. Flat. In the middle of the street. Felt the crunch as blood gushed from my broken nose.

"Oh, baby," said Holly, towering over me. At least eleven feet tall. "Baby's had one too many." She hoisted me from the street like a rag doll, 185 pounds of dead weight, and held me upright. "Holly's going to take you home, baby, and fix you up. Don't worry about one little thing."

Blood gushed ruinously down my shirtfront, one of the last six good shirts I had, worn especially so Fanelli wouldn't think I was totally pathetic. Now I only had five. A Sea Island cotton shirt and blood are not friends.

For a fleeting moment I thought of the squalor of my apartment—the dishes in the sink from last week's attempt at cooking, the dirty shirts and socks, the rats—and then I thought, oh, what the hell. She's a $50 hooker. She's seen it all. I let her drag me to my apartment building's street door, on which the lock was broken, and somehow we made it up the five flights of stairs to my apartment.

After three inept tries with my key, I had to let Holly open the door. She took one look inside and said, "Baby! What explosion happened here!?" Everything Holly said had an exclamation point after it, as though she had just discovered a new planet or a new law of thermodynamics. Baby! The kitchen! Where's the bathroom! Do you have any cotton balls! The idea that I would have cotton balls is kind of like the idea of Marie Antoinette having blue jeans. Not likely.

"What a dump! A nice young man like you! Why do you live here amidst this ruination!?" Holly's way of speaking, like Holly herself, was wholly manufactured, out of old movies and romance magazines.

Meanwhile she was rushing around, stuffing toilet paper up my nose to stanch the bleeding, wiping my face with a clean washrag she miraculously found, getting me out of my shirt. "My God, what a stomach!" she exclaimed. I did three hundred and fifty sit-ups a day to maintain a vestige of what the trainer had worked so hard to create. My body, once a work of art, was collapsing, atrophying, but I did what I could. Push-ups, one fifty. It passed the time, of which there was an infinite amount, even given the amount of time I spent reading Proust, and it made me feel that, when the call came, this soldier would be ready to answer. Not that any calls came, except from Mr. McDermott and Ms. Willoughby, of their respective collection agencies, and others of their ilk, but I kept up the habit. Sometimes, I put them on speakerphone, and did sit-ups while they told me of all the dire things that were about to happen to me. I didn't mind talking to them. They were sort of pleasant, actually. It passed for conversation in the Proustian silence.

Holly was the first real person who had been in my apartment in months. Not that Holly was a real person, as I had heretofore understood the term. Holly was an imagined creation, from the ground up, not real in any way, in the strictest sense. The whole point of being Holly, I suppose, was to outsmart reality, to become something wholly other.

I finally stopped bleeding. Holly helped me to the bed, first straightening the sheets and plumping the pillows. I offered her one of Fanelli's crisp hundreds, 20 percent of my entire worldly goods, and she said, "What do I look like? A nurse! Keep your money, baby! What's your name anyway?"

I mumbled a response.

"That your real name?"

"It's what people call me . . ."

"You really need a cleaning woman or something! A mammy!" she said. "Man was not meant to live like this." I passed out, and when I woke up in the dead of night, bleeding again all over my pillow, Holly was gone, and the apartment was as clean as my apartment was ever going to get. Dirty shirts in the hamper. Shoes put away. Dishes done. A big lipstick kiss on the bathroom mirror. The bloodied shirt was gone.

I looked out the window, and there she was, strolling under the sputtering streetlights in the middle of the street, swinging her baby-doll purse. Also pink, with rhinestones. A nurse. A hooker. A Good Samaritan. A drag queen.

I didn't see Holly for several nights, but when I did, I walked up to her to thank her for her ministrations. She shrieked as though she had just seen her long-lost father. "Baby! Hold on a sec! I have something for you!" She ran off to some secret cubbyhole she kept somewhere on the street, and returned with a bag from Bergdorf's, and a box with the familiar ribbon around it, in which there was a pristine, brand-new Sea Island shirt exactly my size.

"I couldn't get the blood out from the old one. I scrubbed and scrubbed! Look at these hands! So I bought you one I thought you would like. You can always take it back for another one. If you don't, like, like it, I mean."

"Holly," I said, "it's too much. You shouldn't . . ."

"You don't understand a thing, do you! Money means nothing to us girls. To me at least. I'm like a walking bank! They stick it in, and out comes money, and it never stops!" She opened her purse to show me the wads of balled-up cash. "It's virtually endless! I'm a human ATM machine! Open twenty-four hours a day!"

It was a beautiful shirt, and it had been so long since I had a new anything I almost wept. I thanked her, the thanks seeming paltry and inadequate beside her generous gesture, and then the thought of Holly in Bergdorf's hit me, the unlikelihood of it all, of any mercantile exchange happening between Holly and one of the sad, splendid salesmen.

"Honey, when I die just lay me out at Bergdorf's!

Everything is so beautiful there! I just put on my Chanel suit, and yes, I have a Chanel suit, I used to have this, like, boyfriend, well . . ." and a wistful look crossed her face, and she said with dignity, ". . . well, I used to have a boyfriend, and he was so sweet to me, so sweet, and then . . . well, there's always a then, isn't there? Nothing bad could ever happen to you at Bergdorf's! Well, actually, my friend Larice had something bad happen to her but that was only because she had a Halston dress under her coat at the time, and that was bad, but I would never do a thing like that. I bought this shirt with money I earned with my . . . charm and beauty. And now it's yours."

"That's so kind."

"Could we be friends? I don't have any gentlemen friends, and maybe I could come up to your apartment every now and then and warm up. It's cold as a witch's tit out here, and the nights are long and my feet start hurting and . . ."

"Of course. Any time. Although I have to say it makes me a little nervous."

"Of course it does! You're a regular person. I'm like, I'm like a freak of nature! But you'll get used to it. I'm smart. I know a lot of stuff. I'm just not educated. You'll like it, and I won't bother you if you don't want to be bothered. But I will come."

And she did. She did come up to my apartment, not

often at first, but within a month she made an almost nightly visit to see how I was, to describe her lewd and peculiar adventures. I never realized you could do so many extraordinary things in the front seat of a car parked on a dark out-of-the-way street. Sometimes the men would take her to the Hotel Carter, but not often. Usually the encounter was over in fifteen minutes or less, and the men would drop her where they found her and she would follow their taillights as they raced home to safety in New Jersey.

There is such need in the world. It is constant and never changing. It is eternal, and it is worth far more than fifty dollars to find some respite from the hunger and the wanting and the need, so deep it is. We grow engorged and enraged with need, and the relief we find with people like Holly is at best temporary, because the suffocating need is there again in the morning, ravenous and all-consuming. The need was prevalent on Thirty-Fifth Street, sexual desire behind the wheel of every car, real bodies, the flesh, the hairy forearms, the penis, center of gravity for the need that never goes away.

And Holly was there to take it on, the bodies and the pricks and the grasping, hurried hands, the zipper and the smell and the taste, to make the hunger go away for a minute or two, like a snack before dinner, and all she asked was fifty dollars and safe return to her place on the street.

The need died in me when I lost my job, my way, lost

my place in the world, and the romance division of my personal enterprise shuttered its doors forever, and no one has ever gotten in again. My life is my fault. I made it. They did the best they could.

Carmela once asked me, "What is it you really want?"

I shouted at her: "I want to be completely loved and completely left alone!"

But life has taught me in the harshest ways that such a thing is not possible, and so I ended up getting the latter, no matter how much I might need or want the former. Poor Carmela. Such a lovely girl. The sweetheart of my youth.

So I let Holly in for a minute, for a time in my life when there was nothing else, and she would show up, always breathless with news of her adventures, and we would sit and drink Scotch and talk into the night, sometimes with only the light from the television to pierce the darkness. We would drink Scotch and watch almost naked men and women dance ineptly on cable television. The hostess of the show, Robin Byrd, would introduce these dancers as though each were the second coming of Christ, and she would actually interview these morons after they had jerked and slithered their way through two minutes of disco dancing, and they would tout their careers in porn films. Once they even had a she-male like Holly, and as Holly watched she drank her Scotch and made derisive comments. "My breasts are not only bigger, they're masterpieces compared to hers! The best on Park Avenue! Want to see?"

I did not, and Holly seemed to understand and respect this. I was an invalid, in her eyes, and she took care of me like a man dying of cancer, always cleaning, straightening, putting my life back on some kind of recognizably human track. I had lost all bearings.

There was one guy on the TV show, a swarthy Italian guy, Gino or Claudio or something, oiled, massive legs, hairy chest and huge pecs, who was so ripped and built he could barely move, let alone do anything that any sane person would call dancing. He always stopped Holly dead in her tracks, and she would watch his every awkward move with fascination. He was on all the time; apparently he did, like, a porno movie almost every week and always had some product to push. Holly was transfixed, every time.

"He looks exactly like my boyfriend, my one true love!" she said one night. "That's all. My one true time of happiness before I was just another bereft hooker in the street! I had a place, then! I had somebody! Him! Well, not him, but somebody who looked just like him, sort of, if you squint your eyes and don't listen to that disgusting voice."

"We both had somebody, once," I said. "I haven't been like this forever."

"Neither have I. I was somebody with somebody. A

couple, I think they call it. His name was George. Giorgos. Greek. He worked on the printing presses at the *New York Times*. I was sixteen, almost seventeen. I was a boy, then. Just a runaway boy from Cleveland, and George was thirty-three, and he took me in and, man, did he love me. And I guess I loved him back. I was on my own since fourteen, what did I know about love? About anything? When my ride let me off in New York after hitchhiking for five days, I slept on a bench behind the New York Public Library! I thought it was Central Park! Then I stood on the street corner, and I got in the first car that stopped for me, and I did that for two years and one night the car that stopped was George. And I was tired of that life and, well, like, I guess he was just the lucky one. Fate! But I felt for him, in my deepest heart I had feelings for him, and I guess that's love, right?"

"When you feel it, you know it. It's like stepping off a cliff." It was all I could think of to say.

"Can you turn off the TV? I can't watch this and tell the story at the same time. Freaks me out."

I turned it off, and the apartment went from blue to gold, as the light from the streetlight flooded in. Holly moved, ghostlike and golden, around the room, sipping her Scotch. I had never felt so weird in my life. Holly's eyes were moist, as though she was about to cry, and they glistened in the golden light of the room.

"I'm going to tell you this once, and then you're not

going to say anything, and we're never going to talk about it again. OK? Deal?"

"Cross my heart."

"Anyway. Well, anyway." Holly had dropped her usual exclamatory way of talking and spoke from a softer, more vulnerable place. From the heart. From her childish heart, which suddenly seemed, in that odd light and in the deep part of the night, like a lovely thing.

I kept my mouth shut, as I was told.

"He wanted us to live together. He got an apartment in Brooklyn, in a Greek neighborhood, but it was very conservative and he didn't want his neighbors to know he was living with a boy, so I shaved my legs, and put on a blouse and skirt he bought me—he bought me a lot of clothes—and I was a girl. I grew my hair long, and I was pretty, really pretty. It was like I had been waiting all my life to be somebody's girl. I even got a job as a fitting model for Oscar, and I started taking hormone shots. God, it's hot in here!"

As she talked, she began to remove her clothes, piece by piece, and I didn't object, until finally she was naked in her heels, and I saw the whole thing, the deal, what it was like to be Holly underneath her clothes. She made no mention of it, I guess whores are used to taking their clothes off. It was both bizarre and beautiful, in its way. Maybe a trick of the light. The other. The entirely other.

"He found the doctor. He arranged everything. I loved having breasts. He liked big ones, so he found a plastic surgeon and bought the finest pair on the East Coast. And things were so nice for a while. So nice. He was the sweetest man, and I loved everything about him. I loved to feel the weight of him on me in the night, his kisses, like garlic and cigarettes, but sweet somehow. He was a real man. He was a fierce kisser. It was like being devoured by some wild beast. Heaven." Her mascara was starting to run down her face, and she looked, even in the golden light, like she was a million years old.

"He was very traditional. He wanted to get married. Which meant I had to have the operation. He saved his money, and he arranged it all with Dr. Money at Johns Hopkins, and eventually he put me on a Greyhound bus for Baltimore with ten thousand dollars in my little purse.

"But I met these divine sailors in the bus station, and we went for a drink, and one thing led to another, and I woke up a month later in a $20-a-night fleabag with nothing left. The fleet had sailed. No money. No operation. Still a boy. I had to work the street to get enough money to get back to Brooklyn, and when I got there, he took one look and he beat the living hell out of me, and threw me back on the street where he found me."

She downed her Scotch, and put on her clothes, piece

by piece. "End of story. I'll never fall in love again. Don't get up. I can let myself out."

"I . . ."

"Not one word. Not one. That was the deal. I don't need your pity. God! My makeup is a mess! I'll just be a jiffy, and then I'll go! Back into the fray!" She went into the bathroom and closed the door. When she emerged, her makeup restored, her face was like a hard mask, and she was ready for the rest of her night. I watched her for a long time, walking in the middle of the street, watched as she got into a car and sped off, and was still watching, anxious as a father on Prom night, as the car returned her to her perch.

I felt something for her. It wasn't desire and it wasn't pity. It was affection. Easy and welcomed. And a kind of respect. Whatever it was, it was new, and hard for me to fathom, to sort out, especially since I had seen her naked, ambiguous and sexy in a funny kind of way, so I finished the Scotch and went to bed, troubled. Holly was, well, beautiful. Lovely and nineteen and brave. And she had suffered, and suffered still, and I found a fellowship in that. An odd camaraderie between the two most unlikely souls on the planet. In addition to which, I had a brand-new shirt. Score one for generosity.

We became friends. Who else did we have? We would go to the movies in the afternoons. Holly would show up with a bottle of Cristal, ice cold, and we would drink and laugh until everything else was blanked out and meaningless. We went to a party given by one of Holly's friends, in a loft downtown, and got drunk and watched a fat man lip-synch the entire Barbra Streisand songbook. Or so it seemed. He wore a red sequined dress and held a flashlight beneath his chin to illuminate his face in the darkness of the room. The effect was both comic and ghoulish.

Holly got out the fabled Chanel suit, from the lockers at Penn Station where she kept her wardrobe, and we went to Bergdorf Goodman. The family that owned the store lived in an apartment on the top floor, and Holly and I agreed that that was pretty close to our idea of heaven. Holly looked like any young Park Avenue wife. We looked, in fact, like a happy, well-to-do couple. Which, for that afternoon, exploring every floor of the store, trying things on, being haughty with the sales people, we were.

We didn't care if we looked odd on the street. We took care of each other, in the way friends do, and that was good enough for us, for a time.

The bitter cold began to break up into pieces, like ice in a river, and dissolved into clear and sunny days, chilly at night. Easter was coming. Holly continued to visit almost every night, one night even chastely sleeping for two hours beside me in my bed, on top of the covers, before rushing out into the night.

The night before Palm Sunday, Holly showed up breathless at the door and asked me to lunch the next day at a place in the Village I had never heard of, The Ninth Circle. "They have great burgers!" she said. "And a great jukebox! And treats for the eyes and ears! One o'clock. Be sharp. Something has happened! Something wonderful! I have a great piece of news to tell you! Just great!"

The next day was warm, the first really warm day. Easter was late that year, I guess, but Palm Sunday was warm, and I bathed for church and shaved carefully and put on a seersucker suit, and the shirt Holly had given me. It was lavender, with white pinstripes and a white collar and cuffs; I wore with it a rose-colored tie from the tie museum in my closet. I never wore them anymore. No reason.

I looked like an Easter egg.

Church was the one hour in the week to judge my distance from what I considered to be "The Good," and I wanted to be good. People who have lost everything tend to feel that. I wanted to be a good man and cause no harm. Not anymore. *Primum non nocere,* like a doctor. The past was littered with bodies, wounded. It was packed with insults and extravagances that suddenly seemed unconscionable. So I went, like a good boy, partly loving it, and partly hating it, being the pauper in a sea of rich people.

That Palm Sunday, church seemed to go on forever, and I kept checking my watch. I was the only person in a seersucker suit, the rest of the men were in banker blue or gray, pinstripes, and I sat off to the side, so that no one would touch or speak to me. When the collection plate came around, I had nothing to give, so I pretended to pray until it had passed me by. As soon as I had taken Communion, the body and blood, I raced from the church and caught the train down to the Village, where I found, after some difficulty, the Ninth Circle. It was exactly one o'clock.

I pulled open the metal door and walked, palm frond in hand, into the middle of an aggressively dark and seedy leather bar. In my seersucker suit. It was like When Worlds Collide, except that I was the only inhabitant on my planet. The rest of them were all dressed in various forms of black leather, all kinds of stuff I'd never seen before, straps and chaps and harnesses and black leather jeans with no backs on them, codpieces, a museum of a particular fetish that didn't happen to be mine.

They stared at me, facial hair bristling. They stared hard for a long time. Seersucker. Jesus.

The crowded bar seemed to stretch endlessly into a dark back room, where there were tables covered in red checkered linoleum, and a few lost leather souls downing their Budweisers and eating the much-advertised burgers. I made my way through the long gauntlet of black leather, and sat at one of the tables. No Holly. She didn't show up for another forty-five excruciating minutes, and, when she did, she looked like hell.

Today, she was a boy. Hair tied back, wearing jeans and loafers and a T-shirt that had a line that went from nipple to nipple, underneath which it said, "You must be this tall to ride this ride." No makeup, at least only the ghostlike smear of last night's face. Holly needed a shave.

"Sorry!" she said. "*Quel* night. I rushed out of the house like a madwoman! I didn't want to keep you waiting." I didn't point out that she had, in fact, already kept me waiting for almost an hour.

"Oh! You look so handsome! There was a real man under all that self-pity! Bravo! . . . The greatest thing has happened! The greatest thing ever."

"Holly, tell me."

"I'm in love! I've fallen in love with a real man."

"Holly, that's great! I'm so happy for you. Who's the guy?"

There was an awkward pause while Holly let me think it over just long enough that I knew the answer before she spoke.

"You."

The color must have drained from my face, because Holly took my hands, just for a second, then quickly withdrew and put her hands back in her lap. She spoke quietly, without affectation, and with a great tenderness of feeling. She looked down at the table as she spoke, never looking at me, until the end.

"I'm telling you this because . . . because, like, to me, to me at least, the greatest sin is to love somebody and not tell them. That's the greatest sin."

Then she looked into my eyes, and I saw how deep and gentle was the love she was speaking of.

"Because then, when the person you love walks down the street, or walks into a meeting or a room full of strangers, they don't know that somebody loves them. And that can make all the difference in, like, a person's confidence and stuff, you know?

"I know nothing will happen when I tell you I love you. There's no way. You're regular. I'm, well, whatever I am, I'm not regular. I'm not telling you because of that. I'm just telling you so that, when you hail a cab or answer the phone, when you walk into a roomful of strangers, you'll know that there is somebody in the world who loves you and will always love you, wherever you go, whatever happens, until the end of time. Don't ever forget that. Promise you will never forget that you are loved. " She crossed her heart, and touched one finger to my lips. And then, as quickly as she had come, she was gone.

And I wept. In the midst of all the swarthy, muscled

leather men, with their straps and bristling facial hair, and their collars and their chaps, I sat at the grimy table in the seedy leather bar on West Tenth Street, and I wept until I couldn't cry anymore. And then, with what little dignity I had left, I got up to go. I noticed that one of the patrons, I don't know who, had put a glass of beer in front of me while I was crying my guts out, and I looked around for who to thank, but nobody looked at me, so I took a sip of the beer and then I left the Ninth Circle and walked through the gorgeous spring day, all the way back to Hovel Hall, all the way to Thirty-Fifth Street, all the way to whatever was going to happen for the rest of my life.

Loved. Loved. Loved. Forever. Forever. Forever.

And I never saw Holly again. She never came back to Thirty-Fifth Street to rule the street the way she had every night for years. For months I asked the other girls about her, but they didn't know where she'd gone, or wouldn't say. I hung around the lockers at Penn Station where she kept her clothes, but she never showed up. Leaving me alone. Leaving me completely alone but also completely loved, as I had once asked, so many years before. I was also left with no way to thank her. As if thanks were ever enough.

CHAPTER TWENTY-ONE

The Fall of Princes

❖　❖　❖

The rest is just slow diminution and loss. A waning of the full and effulgent moon of my youth. Not that the bright light of my youth was anything to be proud of. I was a terrible person. I did unkind and sometimes illegal things. I treated women abominably. The remembrance of it causes me to flush with shame and to feel a tightening in my groin.

It was a radiance without warmth, and I thought of nothing but myself in the brightness of the light. Now I try never to think of myself. I try not to think at all, not to dwell, but, sometimes, late at night, it all comes back to me, and I lose myself in the life that might have been, the wife of twenty years, her comforts and distractions. The fractious children, raucous at the holidays, with their tattoos you asked them not to get and their lacrosse sticks they play with in the house, stringing and restringing them, the trips to Paris to stay at the Lutetia. Photograph albums of a life that never quite came to be. It doesn't last long when it comes, but it is vivid, and I am there, not here, not here where I belong. When you lose everything, you don't die. You just continue in ordinary pants with nothing in your pockets.

I gave up sending out résumés, tossed them in the trash. I no longer called the people I had known for years who placed brokers in jobs. There was no point. They never took my calls. I had blotted my copybook in perpetuity, one night of gracelessness in the Russian Tea Room, and everything was gone from my résumé, the loft and arc of it, the elevation and grandeur. My name was *up*, as my grandmother used to say. What I did at thirty-two, how bright, how aggressively promising, had no relevance at thirty-seven. Washed up at the moment I had barely set sail.

I looked through the paper and applied for jobs from the want ads. There was always something wrong, with the job, with me. Sitting with these smug hiring people and answering their ridiculous questions.

"You've been out of work for five years. What were you doing?"

"I was living in Europe."

"How exciting! What did you do?"

"I tried to write a novel. It wasn't any good."

"Do you have retail experience?"

I used to buy and sell the world every day before lunch.

"No."

"Would you think you'd be good at sales?"

"I can sell ice cream to the Eskimos."

"But you've never actually done it."

"No."

"Well, very interesting. We'll be in touch if a position opens up. At the moment there's nothing."

"Then why did you advertise? Why did you call me in?"

"We like to keep abreast of who's out there. Can you use a cash register?"

"A moron could learn to use a cash register in ten minutes."

"You'd be surprised. Well, we'll call."

"No. You won't."

Long pause. "Not with that attitude, we won't. I suggest you take a course in people skills. Or look for a job where you don't have to deal with the public. Like writing bad novels. Good day."

Eventually, I learned to smile and lie my way into a series of temporary jobs. You don't die of embarrassment. Not right away.

I demonstrated food processors, and I was astonishingly good at it after only a few days. I could make perfect bread dough in seconds. I wore a white chef's apron and a paper toque, and I survived by pretending to be somebody else. I sprayed elegant women with overly strong perfume from vaguely erotically shaped bottles. I showed people who had little chance of ever going anywhere how to pack two suits flawlessly in a suitcase. I survived.

But I kept seeing people I knew. They looked at me as though I were in some sort of Halloween costume, or, perhaps, one of the comic interludes in a Christmas pantomime, and sometimes, purely out of pity, they would buy a Cuisinart or a tiny bottle of ridiculously overpriced fragrance. It was an act of kindness that mortified me to the center of my being.

Things fell away from me. My parents died, first my mother, then my father, in quick succession, cancer, mortified at my circumstances, leaving me just enough to shut up Mr. McDermott and Ms. Willoughby. Our parting was quite cordial, actually. I would miss our daily chats. After they stopped calling, days would pass between phone calls.

I miss the rustle and hustle and bang of the floor, the deals happening every half-second, the high fives, the bonus days and the dinners at Frank's. I miss the clothes, the deference of salespeople, the winter in Harbour Island before all the people who go there now knew it was there. I miss my cufflinks—lapis lazuli, hematite, ruby, sapphire—all gone to the Orthodox jewelry dealers on Forty-Fifth Street, one pair at a time. And my watches. I miss invitations to parties. Parties of beautiful people who say witty and aggressive things. Everything, everything in that old life is gone. A young man's life, sold for pennies on the dollar.

But every time I let something go, I felt, yes, a sadness, but I also felt lighter, more free, less tethered to a past I would never get back to. Let them have it.

Life was once only about day and night. Now it's about the number of seconds it takes to get from one end to another.

I finished Proust. It gave me an overriding sense of superiority over the vast majority of mankind. I couldn't read anything else for a year after. Compared to the rich broth of Proust, every other book seemed like lukewarm water in my mouth.

I finally found a real job, thanks to Proust. I got a job as a clerk in one of the big chain bookstores, in part, I think, because the woman who was doing the hiring asked me what my favorite book was, and I said, "There's only one real book ever written, besides the Bible. And that is *Remembrance of Things Past*."

She smiled. "We call it *In Search of Lost Time* now."

"I prefer the old title. Less accurate, but more poetic."

"What are the current top-ten best-sellers in fiction?"

I named them, in order. "You want to know the number of weeks they've been on the list?"

"I trust you. Nonfiction?"

I named them, although not in order.

"Have you ever sold anything? Anything at all?"

And I told her the long list of embarrassing jobs I had endured in the last year. I told her how to pack two suits in your suitcase so they emerge wrinkle-free at the end of your journey.

"When can you start?

"This or any other moment."

"Next Monday?"

"How about tomorrow at nine?"

She smiled the smile I was coming to adore. "We don't open 'til ten. You'd be locked out and lonely, Monsieur Proust."

"Then I'll be here at ten."

And I have been there ever since. At first, I was just a clerk, ringing up books. It was like being in hiding. I was relatively safe from running into people I used to work with, since none of them read anything but the *Wall Street Journal*. You could spot me in the T-shirted masses of other clerks because I always wore a tie. I considered being a bookseller not just a job. I looked on it as an honorable profession.

Now I'm the fiction manager, in charge of picking and choosing, all the ordering, and deciding which books get featured spots in the department. It's a job that requires both caution and bravado, and I like doing it. And I'm good at it.

Sometimes I open or close the store. I have keys. I can go in any time I want. Some days, when it's my duty to open the store, I go in at eight o'clock, just to be alone and smell all those books around me. Each one is a door. Each one is a world.

I recommend books to people, and they read them, and then they come back and tell me what they thought. Most people in the neighborhood know me by name by now, so it's a personal thing. Even with the onslaught of digital books, and all the threats to the book-selling business, there are people who still like the heft and feel of a real book, who like having a stack of books by their bedside tables, waiting to be read. Our store is under siege, now, but I think we'll be OK, at least for long enough for me to finish out my working life.

I finally moved out of Hovel Hall and into a small apartment in the Village. I was lucky to get it. My rent is stable, even though prices in the Village have gone through the roof. Every week, when I change the sheets, I look at the half of the bed that has not been slept in, as pristine as the day the sheets were changed, and I wonder what happened to the possibilities of my youth. No one has ever slept in that bed but me, and I have only slept on one side of it.

In the same chaste, deathlike position every night. All those years. All those years that have passed, in the utter silence of that apartment—silent except for the clink of a knife against a fork, the shutting of a cabinet door, the opening of an envelope.

My one extravagance is sheets. They are fine percale cotton, simple but exquisite, and I have them washed and pressed by a Chinese lady in the neighborhood. It doesn't cost that much, and it is a dying art, pressing a sheet perfectly. Jackie Onassis, they say, had her sheets changed twice a day; once when she got up in the morning, and again after her nap. Imagine.

I am not that extravagant, but ironed sheets is one thing I insist on. My last, my only extravagance. At night, on Mondays when I change the sheets, when I get into my freshly made bed, when I feel and smell the crisp percale, I think of it all, and I am perfectly happy.

And I am still loved. I always will be loved. On the street. In a roomful of strangers. Walking up the stairs at the opera, which I attend twice a year, unnoticeable in the jeweled crowd. When I go on a cruise every five years, a single face in that happy crowd of couples, I know something they don't know. I am loved. Holly gave me that, and it cannot be taken away. I have never forgotten. I am loved.

CHAPTER TWENTY-TWO

She Walks in Beauty

❖ ❖ ❖

We were short-handed. We often are, in the summer when it's a good beach day. Come August, a beautiful day, half the clerks call in sick. So I was filling in at the registers. It's so easy now. It hardly takes any thought or skill at all. Everything is done for you. Scan. Swipe. Sign. Transaction over. I can't remember the last time I saw cash.

The hands were lovely, and wore no jewelry at all. Perfect nails. She had two books, popular novels. On top of them was a $50 bill. I looked up, and it was as though no time had elapsed at all since I had last seen her. Not the twenty years it had been. Not a nanosecond. Time, or an assembled team of the world's finest surgeons, had been good to her.

Carmela had always been lovely, and there she stood, unambiguously and unimaginably more lovely than ever. She always said that the secret to growing old gracefully lay in wearing a little less makeup every day, and that morning she had no makeup on at all, her hair tied back in one of those things, tendrils still damp against her neck. I stared at her eyes, glittering like sun reflected on an azure sea. Her hair, once dark, was now streaked with highlights. Women do that as they age, they lighten, become air, their souls ephemeral with memory and experience. Men become more ponderous with the passing of the years, heavy with regret.

"I . . . I just came from Pilates. I never thought . . ."

"You look astonishing. As always."

"I look like a sweaty rat on a barge."

"Queen of the barge rats, then. As ever. I've . . . well I've been thinking—"

"You were never very thoughtful."

"—of you a lot lately. Of those days, and all that happened, all that passed between us, and, well . . . I've just been thinking, is all."

"It went by so quickly. The flare of a match."

"I remember every second of it."

"Was I horrid?" She glanced over her shoulder. "We're holding up the line. They'll riot soon."

"I'll throw them crusts of bread. Have lunch with me. Not horrid. Ever."

"I don't . . ."

"Not for old times sake. I have something I want to say to you. I've been thinking about it for, well, for years, and it has to be said. I never thought the chance would come, but here it is, one in a million. Have lunch with me. I promise, no damage will happen to either one of us."

"Let me just pay for the books . . . Please, Rooney, I . . ."

Nobody had called me that for years. I took her money, our hands touched briefly, and once again, when I put the change in her palm. "I can't . . . let me . . ." she turned to go. The next person stepped forward, but Carmela turned back.

"What time? Where?"

I named one of our favorite restaurants.

"It's been closed for years. Heartrending. Tragic, really."

"Name your favorite."

"Marea. The kind of place we always liked." She spelled it. "Do you know it?"

"No. I'll look it up."

"Central Park South. One o'clock."

I arrived at the restaurant a few minutes early. It was

very fancy, in an austere, cream-colored sort of way. Beautiful people at lovely tables, the room bristling with servers intent on doing one thing at a time exactly correctly. The summer glare from the street softened by curtains of silk gauze, saffron colored.

They put me at an obscure table for two near the kitchen, and I knew Carmela wouldn't like it, but I didn't have the heart or the clout to ask for another. Why would they give it to me? They probably wondered how I had come to wander into their restaurant in the first place, The table was next to the silverware station, and the calm of the room was constantly disturbed by the busboys hurling clean silverware into the drawers, or the waiters more gently taking out what they needed, piece by piece.

She walked in from the torrid day at one fifteen, carrying a shopping bag, and she looked as though she moved in a cloud of air-conditioning. Red shoes, and nobody ever wore red shoes better, a pale, rose-flowered silk dress, carrying a red, wide-brimmed straw hat in her right hand. She looked expensive. Also fresh, perfectly at home in the world, in that way some New Yorkers of means have. Lovely from toe to head, her eyes concealed by dark glasses that she took off with a grace that defies description. A lowering of the head. A lifting of the glasses, revealing the eyes. A slight smoothing of her hair. Stunning.

She spoke graciously to the maître d', who actually

kissed her on both cheeks, and he then led her to me, but decided instantly to change our table to one for four in the center of the restaurant, like the crown jewel. She gracefully laid her red hat on one of the empty place settings, and took no notice of the fuss that was being made of her. A kind of all-encompassing and gracious gratitude pervaded her every gesture. The busboy might have been her long-lost son.

"Hello, Giovanni. How is your mother?"

"Very well, signora. She comes home soon."

"You must miss her."

"I miss her cooking. Flat or sparkling?"

"Sparkling, I think. It's so hot out." He turned to go. "And a glass of champagne. The usual."

She turned to me. "I gather you don't drink anymore."

"Why would you say that? I don't, but how did you know?"

"Because, my sweet, once-upon-a-time husband, that is the arc of your life. Wretched excess followed by pious sobriety."

"I'm hardly pious."

"You'd be the first, in my experience."

"Trust me."

"Sober libertine, then? Did you become a homosexual, as I always thought you would?"

"I did. Not that I march in parades or anything."

"Not Out Loud and Proud?"

"Just not out loud."

"And is it fun, being a homosexual?" Her smile was not in the least sarcastic.

"I'm not very good at it, to tell the truth. I was better with the other. I was a killer with women. How about you?"

"Children, yes. Nicholas, Jack, and Carmela. I couldn't help myself. Husband, not at the moment."

Before I could speak—and I didn't want to speak because we were too quickly falling into the old ways, the thin, heartless badinage—the water appeared and was poured, not a single drop on the pristine tablecloth, and then the waiter came to take our order.

"You'll have the skate?" I asked Carmela.

"Why do you say that?"

"I've never known you not to order the skate whenever it was on the menu."

"That was years ago, darling. Years and years." She turned to the waiter, "I'll have the skate." She turned back to me with a radiant smile full of perfect teeth with which she had not been born.

"I have a present for you." She handed me the shopping bag. Inside was a mink lap robe, lined with chamois. Exquisite. Vastly expensive. At the height of summer. Something told me that somebody else had once given it to Carmela, perhaps as recently as last Christmas.

"I know you were always mad for exquisite bedclothes."

"It's magnificent. Thank you."

"You were saying?"

I put the bag on the floor by my seat. "I wanted to say something. I've been waiting for years to say it, and, when it's said, we can talk about anything you want. Anything but that."

"Your lunch. Your rules." The smile was gone from her face, but not the radiance.

I paused a minute, took a sip of water. I wanted to, had to get this right. This moment would only come once. "I fell in love with you the first time I saw you. *Totalement, completment, tragiquement.* It was at that dinner at my loft. You brought the saber dancers. You had on red shoes, like today, and a red suit, and ruby and diamond earrings. The minute I saw you, I was lost in love. And then things happened as they did, and, for a time, you were mine. You were my world. And then the world fell apart, my fault entirely. But I have never stopped loving you. Not for a minute, not for a second. Never. I love you still."

She sat for a long minute, looking, not at me, but at the chic diners in the exquisite room. Then she turned to me, and the full force of her eyes burned for the last time into my heart. She reached out a hand as though she were about to touch me, on the arm, on the and, and then she withdrew and put her hands in her lap.

She looked at me, then, not with love or passion, but with her whole heart's worth of sympathy and compassion. "I know" was all she said, with a tenderness and a sweetness that would be enough to last a lifetime.

I thought of Holly. I said, "I'm telling you this because the greatest sin is to love somebody and not to tell your love. If you stay silent, they don't know, when they walk down the street or into a room full of strangers, that they are loved. You are loved, and that can never be taken from you. It's not much. It's all I have. Maybe it's enough."

"I'll hold it in my heart for as long as I live. Thank you." I could tell she meant it genuinely.

The food arrived, and we ate in silence, the way couples who have been married for twenty-five years do. Occasionally one of us would mention the weather, or the baseball season, but never the past, and never the present. We were no longer a part of the conversation we were having. It was just generic talk. We might have been strangers thrown together at a table on a train or a cruise. But it felt nice. Comfortable. I was going to be late getting back to work, but I didn't care.

Carmela had sorbet and an espresso. She didn't rush, and I was grateful for that. I would never see her again, at least not to speak to, and I wanted it all, the flowered silk dress, the carmine hat and shoes, to burn themselves into my mind so I could hold on to every detail forever. And she knew that, she who would pick up the hat and gather her bag and go back to her life, her children, to whatever awaited her that afternoon. Hair appointment. A meeting with a decorator to pick new curtains for the library.

But it couldn't last. It was now after two, and she gathered up her bag and the red hat, and shook my hand in leaving.

I said in parting, "Carmela? It was nice, though, wasn't it? For a while?"

She paused. "It was . . . amusing," she said. "There's a difference."

I watched until she disappeared, Carmela speaking to the maître d', and then walking out the revolving doors and into the sunshine, where she put on her sunglasses and turned toward Fifth Avenue, walking without haste.

When I called for the check, I was told the lady had taken care of everything. Somewhat embarrassed, but also touched, I left forty dollars on the table and went out into the stifling heat and walked back to my job, to the book-store, to the whole of my ordinary life.

The next day, I went to a jeweler and bought a wedding ring. On the inside, I had engraved "Love Always— Carmela." I wear it because when I do, people on the street can look at me and see that there is some woman in this world who loves me enough to marry me. It gives me comfort, and a certain sense of pride.

And, on some days, certain good days, or some nights when I slip into my crisp and perfect sheets, I almost believe it.

Love always.

Carmela.

CHAPTER TWENTY-THREE

Coda

❖ ❖ ❖

We were closing the store for the night. It was my night to lock up. One of the young employees, this marvelous girl named Tara who had every kind of tattoo and piercing available on the planet, was restocking the shelves, but she was totally inept at it, and so I pitched in, and finished in minutes what it would have taken her another hour to do.

We checked the café on the third floor for any bums or homeless people who might be hiding out there for the night, but found nobody. Not tonight. As I was turning out the lights, Tara turned to me and said, with enormous admiration, "Man, you really, like, know what you're doing."

I turned to her. "'My name is Ozymandias, king of kings: Look on my works, ye Mighty, and despair.'"

"What?" she said. "Could you say that again?"

Acknowledgments

This book was intended as a paean to a city that no longer exists, and a tour of a magical and lethal landscape for those who never knew it. It was marvelous, rich, and dynamic, and in it lived the sweethearts and the darlings of my youth. Some were destroyed, but most were not, and to all, both living and dead, I offer this scrapbook of our youth. It would not have been written had their memories not stayed so clear and cherished in my heart. I embrace them all.

Anne and Mame Kennedy, sisters who came and conquered, Peter Nadin, Katherine Rayner Johnson, who moved me to love her profoundly at first sight, in every detail down to the red shoes, and whose memory is alive and with me every day, may she live forever, Ty French and Rick Grimaldi, gone savagely and too soon, though not uncared for, Dale Engelson Sessa, who found her prince, Shirts, who once told me, "A clean bar is a happy bar," good words to live by, Holly Woodlawn, who left me knowing that I would never in my life be fully alone, David Gould, a king and a priest and a true and good friend unlike any other, Jeanne Voltz and The Dutchman, Catherine and David Dunn, Eugene Orza, Nancy and Bonnie Axthelm, the Sisters Karamozov, Bob and Lynn who came and never left, whom I admire and thank every day with all my heart, and, of course, Hazel and Mariah, Susan Sarandon, who illuminates far many more lives than my own, Jean Pagliuso, Tommy Cohen, Diane Sokolow, John Loeffler, Kathleeen Seltzer and Diana Van Fossen, two more graceful creatures never walked the earth, Larry and Penny Bach, Sally and Larry Mann, Tommy Spencer, Nora Champe Leary, Dana Hoey, Jan Groover, who showed me finally what I looked like, Dan Zanes, who saved my life, Alexandra Como Saghir, so many, so many . . . if I have forgotten to mention you, do not think you are forgotten, their names and faces and voices fill my mind at random moments every day, and my love for them endures everything—the changing of the times, the fluctuations of fortune, the cruelties of age. In my mind they are happy and well and alive. I hope I die before they do. To live without them would be unbearable.

Also, for Lynn Nesbit and Ellen Goldsmith-Vein. I hope and trust they know why.

And, of course, for Guy Trebay, who knew and survived the city far better than I, with grace and brilliance, and whose genius for friendship surpasses any I have ever known. More anon.